THE GOVERNOR'S DOG IS MISSING!

SLATE ✦ STEPHENS ⭐#1 M✦Y✦S✦T✦E✦R✦I✦E✦S

THE GOVERNOR'S DOG IS MISSING!

Sneed B. Collard III

www.buckinghorsebooks.com

Distributed by Mountain Press Publishing Company, Missoula, Montana
1-800-234-5308
www.mountain-press.com

Cover and Book Design by Kathleen Herlihy-Paoli, Inkstone Design.
The text of this book is set in New Century Schoolbook.
It is printed on 100% post-consumer waste paper.

Collard, Sneed B.
        The governor's dog is missing! / by Sneed B. Collard
III. -- 1st ed.
        p. cm. -- (Slate Stephens mysteries ; #1)
        LCCN 2010914110
        SUMMARY: Recounts the humorous and dramatic
adventures of twelve-year-old sleuths Slate Stephens and
Daphne McSweeney as they scramble to find Cat, the
Governor of Montana's missing dog.
        ISBN-13: 978-0-9844460-1-8
        ISBN-10: 0-9844460-1-X

        1. Dogs--Juvenile fiction. 2. Politics, Practical--
Montana--Juvenile fiction. 3. Montana--Juvenile
fiction. 4. Detective and mystery stories. [1. Dogs--
Fiction. 2. Politics, Practical--Fiction. 3. Montana--
Fiction. 9. Mystery and detective stories.] I. Title.
II. Series: Collard, Sneed B. Slate Stephens mysteries ; #1.

        PZ7.C67749Gov 2011   [Fic]
                                QBI10-600199

Manufactured in Canada

10 9 8 7 6 5 4 3 2 1

Bucking Horse Books
MISSOULA, MONTANA

To my sister Meghann, a passionate animal lover.

Love, Sneed

One

Half a dozen partly-digested Nutty Nuts spew out of my mouth. They splatter against the newspaper I hold and slowly slide like mucous-covered slugs toward my lap.

"No way!" I exclaim.

There, right above the slime-coated Nutty Nuts, today's *Helena Gazette* headline shouts:

Governor's Dog Missing!

I quickly scan the story's first few paragraphs and glance at my sister across the table from me.

"Lily," I say. "Someone took Governor Rickson's dog!"

My sister looks up from a three-inch plastic figure of Donald Duck. She smiles and says, "I pooped yesterday."

Did I mention Lily is only three years old? The age at which life revolves around candy, Disney, and "the potty"?

I don't bother replying. Instead, I shove one last spoonful of cereal into my mouth and, clutching the newspaper, rush up to my bedroom. I shed my pajamas, throw on shorts, shoes, and a T-shirt, and gallop back down the stairs—almost bowling over my mom ahead of me.

"Hey! What's the hurry?" she shouts as I dodge past her and vault the last four steps to the first floor landing.

"I'm going to Daphne's!"

"Don't forget your science class at—"

But the screen door has already slammed shut behind me.

I race up the block to Daphne's house and bound up onto her porch. It is a gorgeous summer day, but I hardly notice the sun and endless blue sky above me. Instead, I rap my knuckles hard against the door.

From inside the house, violin music is playing, but it suddenly stops and I hear adult footsteps approach. The door swings open and Daphne's mom Theresa stands before me, bow in hand.

She smiles. "Good morning, Slate. What are you up to today?"

"Sorry I interrupted you," I pant. "Is Daphne in?"

"It's okay," Theresa says. "I'm just rehearsing for the summer concert this weekend." Then, she turns and yells up the stairs, "DAAA-PHneee! Slate is here!"

"Send him up," I hear Daphne's voice call down.

Her mom steps aside and points her bow. "You know the way."

"Thanks." I gallop up the stairs and burst into

the first room on the right. I find Daphne hanging upside down from a bar attached to her closet doorframe.

I halt. "What are you *doing*?"

She yanks her shirt up to cover her belly button. "I'm getting more oxygen to my brain."

"By hanging upside down?"

"It sends the blood to my head."

She tries to pull herself back up to the bar, but can't do that and keep her shirt up at the same time.

"Turn around!" she commands, her face the color of an organically-grown grape.

I obey and hear a thump on the floor. Then, I spin around and shove the newspaper in her face.

"Have you seen *this*?"

Two

Daphne focuses on the paper. "Let's see...Grizzlies Tear Up Glacier Park Campground... Legislators Grumble Over Special Session on Educa—"

"Not *those* stories." I seize the newspaper and flip it around to the top half. "*That!*"

"Oh."

I pace the room while Daphne reads the lead story. Before she's even finished, I blurt, "Can you believe someone stole Cat?"

And you did hear me right about the dog's name. Before going into politics, our governor farmed wheat and raised sheep outside of Fort Benton, in north-central Montana. He's also known to have a passion for buying heavy equipment. Newspaper photos always show him racing around on his latest bulldozer or super-charged tractor. Apparently, he named his Border collie "Cat" after his favorite Caterpillar brand backhoe. I mean, who wouldn't, right?

In any case, Cat has easily become the most famous dog in Montana. Governor Rickson takes him everywhere. You can hardly find a photograph or watch a T.V. news story about the governor without seeing Cat in it, too. Last year for a homework assignment, my sixth-grade English teacher gave us the choice of writing a letter to the governor or writing to Cat instead. Everyone but Seth Hardrake and Riley Norbaum wrote to Cat. We got a letter back, along with a poster of Governor Rickson and Cat posing on—what else?—a tractor.

Daphne finally lowers the newspaper. "It doesn't say Cat was *stolen*," she tells me. "It just says that he disappeared yesterday during the governor's morning walk."

She pauses to pick at the newsprint with her fingernail. "Are these pieces of Nutty Nuts cereal?"

I ignore her question. "So," I say, "if the dog wasn't stolen, what could've happened to him?"

Daphne plops down on her bed. By this time her face has returned to its normal color, and she sweeps a strand of her black hair over her ear. Something about the way she does it makes my heart do a little skip. This isn't the first time that's happened lately, but I tell myself that I'm just excited from the run over here.

"Cat could be missing for a lot of reasons," Daphne says. "Dogs often get lost."

"A Border collie? I don't think so. Border collies are one-person dogs. Cat never would have drifted far enough away from Governor Rickson to get lost. And even if he did, he would have come back."

Daphne frowns. "Okay then. He could have gotten run over by a car."

"Wouldn't someone have found the body by now?"

Daphne gives me her impatient look—the one where she draws her lips back like an irritated frog.

"Well, Mr. Genius," she says. "Instead of just shooting down *my* ideas, why don't you try coming up with your own? And don't give me some big conspiracy theory. No one would have kidnapped the cat—uh, I mean, Cat the dog."

"Why not? People take dogs and cats all the time. I read online about people who steal dogs and cats to teach them to communicate telepathically. They use them to spy on terrorists."

"Oh, come on! What website were you reading, *stories-for-idiots.com*?"

"Noooo," I say, defensively. I don't want to tell her I found it on a website called "PseudoScience."

"Just shows you can't believe everything on the Web," Daphne tells me.

"Hmph."

We sit there in silence for a few seconds. Then, Daphne turns to me, her face more serious. "What if Cat is lying injured in a ditch where no one can see him? What if he's trapped somewhere?"

I nod, imagining a dog of mine lying hurt and alone. A sense of urgency fills me. "We should go see if we can help find him."

Three

Daphne and I have only been in Helena for two weeks, but have already figured out the transportation system. We're used to figuring stuff out. Our fathers are both research geologists at the University of Montana in Missoula. They work together on different studies all around Montana. This summer they're working on—well, we can talk about that later. The point is that this year, our families are spending the summer in Helena's old mansion district. It's a neighborhood full of historic homes—Victorians, bungalows, huge brick houses with fancy turrets and low stone walls surrounding them. A forest of ash trees lines the streets.

After leaving Daphne's house, we hurry several blocks to the nearest trolley stop. We arrive just in time to see the red-and-white bus, made up to look like an old-fashioned trolley, growling toward us. We show the driver our summer passes and look out the window as the trolley winds its way through downtown. Ten minutes later, it dumps us out right in front of Montana's most spectacular building, the Capitol.

"So, where do we start?" I ask, looking up at the

sunlight glinting off the grayish-green Capitol dome.

"Well," Daphne says. "The newspaper article said Cat disappeared during the governor's morning walk."

"Okay, let's go," I say, starting off down the sidewalk.

"Hello? Slate?" Daphne calls.

I stop and turn. "What?"

"Do you already *know* where the governor walks his dog every morning?"

"Well, no. But it's got to be around here, right?"

Daphne looks at me patiently. "Don't you think it might help if we found out?"

I growl. "And how should we do that, All-Knowing One?"

"This may sound crazy and out of this world, but I thought that maybe we could go to the Governor's Office and ask."

Daphne has a point. Instead of admitting it, however, I just turn and begin walking up to the Capitol. And even though I've seen it from a distance a dozen times already, I can't help feeling a flush of pride looking at the grandiose building before me.

As any Montana school student knows—or should know if he doesn't spend his days peeling gum off the bottom of his desk—Helena wasn't actually Montana's original capital. The gold rush towns of Bannack and Virginia City first ruled the territory. When Montana became a state in 1889, two of Butte's famous "Copper Kings" duked it out over where the new capital should be. By hook—and more than a little crook—Helena came out on top.

Daphne and I enter the capitol building through a set of glass doors that look like they lead into a basement, but is actually the Capitol's first floor. We pass a guard station and expect to be x-rayed or strip-searched, but the guard doesn't even glance at us. It's a good thing. My braces would have set off alarm bells for miles in every direction.

"Now what?" I ask.

Daphne and I glance down low-ceilinged, dim hallways that lead in opposite directions. Even though I've seen the building from a distance, I've never actually been inside of it, and I'm thinking that the Capitol's interior isn't nearly as impressive as its exterior.

Daphne walks up to the guard station.

"Excuse me, sir. Do you know where the Governor's Office is?"

The guard glances up from the book he is reading, a thick paperback titled *Total Destruction*.

"Second Floor, East Wing. Up the stairs," he tells us.

We hurry up the staircase in front of us. Then we turn, take a few steps, and halt.

Our jaws drop.

On every side, fancy columns, arches, and alcoves rise two stories above us. Above that, the inside of the capitol dome soars so high, I feel like I'm either about to ascend to heaven or get sucked into one of those wormholes that spaceships travel through in sci-fi movies.

"Wow," Daphne and I whisper at the same time.

Daphne's brought her camera along and raises the viewfinder to her eye to snap a couple of photos. It's not hard to see why. Paintings and bronze busts adorn every wall, nook, and cranny around us. Polished wood railings and gleaming tile floors give the elegance of a palace.

"Who are those guys?" I whisper, pointing to four especially impressive round paintings looking down on us. One is an Indian chief, another a mountain man. I can't figure out what the other two guys are.

"I don't know," says Daphne, lowering her camera, "but that looks like the Governor's Office down there."

I pull my eyes from the dizzying space, and follow Daphne down a short marble-lined hallway to a set of double wood-and-glass doors. Above them, gold lettering on another glass panel reads "Office of the Governor."

We step past American and Montana flags into a large suite of offices. A young man looks up from a reception desk. "Can I help you?"

"Um, we heard about the governor's dog," I tell the receptionist. "We want to help look for him."

The man smiles. "That's very nice of you, but

believe me, every available law enforcement person in Helena is keeping an eye out."

"Oh."

Daphne steps forward. "That's great news," she says, "but a couple of extra pairs of eyes wouldn't hurt would they?"

The man hesitates and says, "Uh, just a minute."

He gets up and walks into a nearby room. A moment later, he returns with a woman about our parents' age. She sticks out her hand.

"I'm Sheila Russo, the Governor's Deputy Chief of Staff."

Daphne and I glance at each other, eyes wide. We shouldn't really be surprised. One of the great things about Montana is that it's a place where you can meet anybody at almost any time—even the Governor's Deputy Chief of Staff. I mean, try doing that in Texas or New York.

We shake Ms. Russo's hand and give her our names.

"So," she says. "I hear you want to help find Cat."

Daphne recovers her wits first. "Yes. I mean, we don't really expect to find him ourselves, but we thought that maybe we could retrace Governor Rickson's walking route. Poke into a few corners and maybe pick up some clues other people might have missed."

Ms. Russo nods. "Sounds like a good plan. What exactly can I do for you?"

"We were wondering if you could tell us where the governor and Cat walk every morning?"

"I can do better than that. Follow me." The Deputy Chief of Staff leads us into her office. She walks around to her desk and pulls out a pad of printed maps of Helena and tears one off. She takes out a highlighter and we move in closer.

"The governor always starts his walk at the governor's residence here," Ms. Russo tells us, drawing an orange 'X' at a location about two blocks away. She proceeds to trace Governor Rickson's route through nearby neighborhoods, over to a local coffee shop downtown, ending up back at the capitol building itself.

"So Cat actually does come to work with him?" I ask.

"Every day. Would you like a photo of Cat?"

Daphne and I have both seen dozens of pictures of the governor's dog, but I say, "Sure."

Ms. Russo reaches back into her drawer and pulls out an eight-by-ten glossy of Governor Rickson and Cat sitting on a huge threshing machine.

"Perfect. Thank you for all your help," Daphne says.

"Yeah, thank you," I say.

"The Governor appreciates *your* help," Ms. Russo tells us.

We say goodbye to the Deputy Chief of Staff and leave her office. As we're passing the receptionist's desk, though, Daphne pauses. "Thank you *so much* for your help," she gushes at the young man.

Startled, the receptionist says, "Oh, don't mention it."

"It was a *big* help." Daphne smiles, making herself look as pretty as possible.

I scowl. She doesn't have to try very hard.

Four

I stomp my way back out of the Capitol, but am not exactly sure why. Daphne takes no notice.

"Everyone was so *nice*," she says. "Even the receptionist."

"Jerk," I mutter, my brain set on "Broil".

Daphne looks at me. "What did you say? Stop mumbling."

"I *said* that *of course* he was helpful the way you were…were…flirting with him."

Daphne halts, mouth open. "*Flirting?* Slate, that is the stupidest thing I've ever heard you say."

"Whatever." I continue stomping down the sidewalk.

Daphne hurries to catch me. Her frown breaks into a grin.

"You're jealous!"

I wheel on her. "I am not! For all I care, you can flirt with every receptionist in Montana—and Wyoming, too! I just thought we were here to find the governor's dog—not a *boyfriend* for you!"

Daphne laughs, which makes me even madder. "Slate, he's in his *twenties*! Why would I be flirting with *him*?"

"Well, apparently you'll flirt with anyone, won't you?"

I bat my eyelashes in imitation, hoping this will spike Daphne's anger meter. Instead, her mouth just settles into a smile.

"I'm sorry, Slate. I didn't know I was flirting."

"You were."

"Or that I was making you jealous."

"Jeal—" I begin to shout, but then catch myself. "Let's just find Cat, okay?"

"Fine with me," Daphne says, tossing her black hair behind her.

By the time we reach the governor's house, or the "executive residence" as it's called, I've cooled down a little—though I'm still not sure why I got so mad in the first place. "So, where do we start?" I ask, trying to shake off whatever it was that just happened.

Daphne looks at the map and then twists it around to orient herself.

"Well, when Governor Rickson leaves the front door, it looks like he heads west, toward downtown," she says, nodding along a street called Broadway.

"Okay," I say. "Let's go."

As we walk, a steady stream of cars zips past us. We walk about half a mile, looking into yards and glancing down side streets. We pass a green-painted elementary school and Daphne says, "You know. There's a lot of traffic on this street. If Cat were any- where along here, someone would have reported him."

"Let's cut over a couple of blocks," I tell her.

We can actually cut over only one block, up a hill to a street where the houses are older than they are around the Capitol. It's a lot more peaceful here than on Broadway.

"You look on this side of the street. I'll check the other side," I say.

"Good idea," Daphne says.

"CA-AAAT!" I yell.

"CA-AAAT!" Daphne shouts from across the street.

After a couple of blocks, I meet an older man out for a walk.

"You out lookin' for the governor's dog?" he asks me.

"Yeah. Are you?"

"I'm keepin' my eye out. So's everyone else around here," the man says, waving his hand down the street. "But I don't think he's here. If he was, we woulda seen him by now."

Daphne joins us from across the street.

"Does everyone know what Cat looks like?" she asks, holding the picture for the man to see.

The man chuckles. "Sure. The Guv often walks down this street instead of Broadway. We see them together all the time."

Daphne looks at the map and then raises an eyebrow at me. I nod. We are both thinking the same thing. After the man moves on, Daphne says,

"So, Governor Rickson *doesn't* actually follow the same route every day."

"No," I agree. "He's *peripatetic*."

I grin at Daphne, seeing if I've stumped her with the word. It's a game we've played since we met. Since we're both big readers, we're always trying to find words the other person doesn't know.

Daphne looks at me and says, "You are peri-pathetic."

I give her shoulder a shove. "Ha! You don't know what it means, do you?"

"You wish. It means to *perambulate*. To wander around."

I grunt. "You're guessing. I can tell."

"The point is," Daphne says, waving her hand impatiently, "Cat might be someplace no one is looking for him."

"What should we do?"

We stand on the sidewalk thinking for a few moments.

"Let's finish tracing the governor's basic route," Daphne says. "Then, we can decide if we want to go back and look more in certain places."

"Sounds good. Where to next?"

Daphne consults the map. "This way."

We continue walking west, again following Broadway. Suddenly, as we reach the historic downtown area, I spot a medium-sized black-and-white dog about a block ahead of us. The dog is sniffing at a fence post and for a split second I think I'm imagining it. But then, I squint my eyes and grab Daphne's arm.

"Look!"

"Look at what?"

I point. "There!"

At first, Daphne doesn't see it. Then her eyes focus.

"That's not..." she begins, but doubt creeps into her voice. "Is it?"

We hurry forward. My heart is galloping, thinking it can't possibly be the governor's dog. On the other hand, it sure *looks* like the governor's dog.

As we get to within half a block, I am growing more and more certain that the dog is Cat. But then, the dog notices us coming toward it. In an instant, it turns tail and dashes away.

"After him!" I shout.

Five

Daphne and I race down the street. By the time we reach the corner, the dog has disappeared. Our eyes dart in every direction.

"There he is!" Daphne shouts, pointing to a trail up a nearby hillside.

After a quick check for traffic, we sprint across the street and up the hill. The hill is part of a little park with an old wooden fire tower on its top. We see the dog reach the fire tower and run hard after it. By the time we arrive at the tower, however, the dog has again vanished.

"Where is he?" I shout frantically.

"CAAA-AT!" Daphne calls. She runs around the tower one way while I run around it the other. We meet on the far side.

"Did you see him?" I pant.

Daphne shakes her head, and we each spin around several times, our eyes pinballing across the landscape.

The dog is gone.

"Do you think that was Cat?" I ask.

"I'm not sure," Daphne answers, pulling out the photo, so we can both look at it.

"Same color."

"Same size."

We both let out heavy sighs.

"Now what?" I ask.

Since we're here anyway, we decide to take a closer look at the fire tower. We've both seen it plenty of times—almost daily, in fact, since we arrived in Helena—but this is the first time we've been up close.

A black iron fence surrounds the landmark. Looking through the fence to a metal plaque, we read that the tower was built in 1876 after a huge fire converted downtown Helena into a giant ashtray. The tower was manned twenty-four hours a day to keep disaster from striking again, and has this cool octagon-shaped perch for the fire sentries. More important, the hill that it's on gives Daphne and me a bird's eye look at downtown.

"Well, at least it's a nice view from up here," Daphne says, taking a couple of photos, then checking them on the LCD screen to see that they came out how she wanted.

From here, we can see almost all of the historic downtown area, from Last Chance Gulch all the way up to the Great Northern Town Center and Carroll College beyond that. It's easy to trace a lot of the governor's morning walking route.

"Now, where would you hide out if you were Cat?" Daphne muses.

"I wouldn't hide anywhere," I tell her. "Like I

said, Border collies don't just wander off. They stick close to their masters."

"How do you even know that?" Daphne challenges me. "You don't have a dog."

"We used to," I tell her. "And she was a Border collie."

Daphne's hazel eyes catch the light from the sky. "You never told me you had a dog."

"Her name was Gneiss."

"You mean Nice with an 'n', or the rock gneiss with a 'g'?"

"Take a wild guess."

Daphne gives the cute little snort that she does. "I know who named her *that*."

"Yeah. My dad said she had spots that made her look like gneiss or granite." I laugh. "Whenever we'd call her name, other people thought we were just calling like 'nice doggie.'"

"What happened to her?"

"She died right before our dads started working together."

"I'm sorry."

I shrug, but can still feel an ache in my chest almost five years later.

Neither of us talk for a moment. Then, Daphne says, "I know what will help us crack this case."

I look over at her. "What?"

"A stop at the Parrot."

I grin. "You are exactly right."

Six

Descending the hill from the fire tower, we drop into the walking mall that forms the top of Last Chance Gulch. I already know how this street got its name. I'm one of those weird kids who actually reads guidebooks before I go to a new place. Pretty nerdy, huh?

Anyway, the guidebook explained that, like a lot of other Montana cities, Helena owes its existence to a lucky strike. The story goes that in 1864, four forlorn prospectors were panning for gold in the area and had been totally skunked. They were just about to give up and buy wagon train tickets back home, but decided to give it one "last chance." Right where the old downtown sits today, the prospectors saw that magical yellow glint in their pans. Their find helped turn Helena into one of the richest towns in the West.

As Daphne and I pass historic brick buildings, I try to imagine what Helena was like when it was a ramshackle frontier town full of saloons, gambling halls, and miners in desperate need of soap, deodorant, and mouthwash.

But then, a large crowd interrupts my thoughts.

"What's going on?" Daphne asks.

Right in front of the Parrot, about fifty people

crowd around an unhappy-looking man in a blue suit and red tie. Two T.V. crews film the man as reporters shove microphones into his face.

"That guy looks familiar," I say, as we join the crowd. "Do you recognize him?"

Daphne shakes her head.

A woman in front of us turns and whispers, "That's State Senator Futzenburg."

"Oh, yeah," Daphne says. "We learned about him when we were studying state government last year. He's the Minority Party Leader isn't he?"

"That's right," the woman tells us.

"Shh!" someone hisses.

Daphne and I stand on our toes to get a better look at the senator and hear what he's saying—or *yelling*, that is.

"—this special session is a total waste of tax-payer money!" State Senator Futzenburg shouts into the microphones. "Montana has one of the best education systems in the entire country, and like my Daddy always told me, if somethin' ain't broke, why in blazes should we try to fix it?"

Daphne and I smile at each other. The senator is famous across Montana for quoting wisdom from his Daddy.

"No," the senator continues, "this special session is just another stunt by the governor and the Majority Party to get attention and suck money from the wallets of honest Montanans!"

"But isn't it true," a reporter asks, "that Montana pays starting teachers lower wages than every other state except Wisconsin and South Dakota? And that in many national education rankings, Montana ends up near the bottom of the list?"

"Statistics!" Senator Futzenburg shouts, his face glowing like a wood-burning stove. "Statistics don't mean a thing. Besides, I read a report that lists Montana students as the *seventh smartest* in the entire country! I visit schools all the time and I can tell you, we've got some of the brightest kids in the entire world right here in the Treasure State!"

"So shouldn't we be willing to spend a little more money on them?" another reporter asks.

"We spend *millions* on them every year!" the senator responds. "Besides, how helpful will an education be if our Montana parents can't afford groceries? Tell me that! As my Daddy always said, 'Bread first. Brains second.'"

Daphne and I both burst out laughing at this last remark. So do several other people in the crowd. Even the senator is forced to smile, but he quickly gets back on track. "No, I say again, this special session is just an attempt by the governor to boost his ratings for the next election. Any other questions?"

One of the reporters asks, "Senator, do you have any thoughts on the governor's missing dog?"

Senator Futzenburg growls. "That *dog*. What's his name? Elk or Squirrel, something like that?"

The crowd chuckles.

"Cat," a reporter tells him.

"Right. Cat. Crazy name for a dog if you ask me."

"What do you think happened to him?" the reporter presses.

The senator flinches at the question. "How should I know?" he blusters. "If it were up to me, dogs would be kept out of politics all together. Only reason the governor even got elected was because of that darned dog. Doesn't surprise me someone would take him."

A murmuring sweeps through the crowd.

"You think someone *stole* Cat?" the reporter asks.

"I didn't say that!" the senator sputters. "Again, how should I know what happened? Furthermore, is it really all that important? If we spent more time giving Montana taxpayers a break and less time worrying about lost dogs, this state would be a whole lot better off!"

Seven

Seated inside the Parrot, I lean across the table toward Daphne. "Did you hear that?" I whisper. "Senator Futzenburg said someone stole Cat!"

"He didn't *say* that someone stole him. He *intimated* it." Daphne says, throwing her own vocabulary word my way.

"Yeah. Yeah," I tell her. "He implied or suggested it. I know. If you're going to test me, at least give me a word that's challenging."

"I wasn't testing you," she lies, tracing her finger in a circle while we wait for chocolate milkshakes. "My point is that you thought Cat was stolen, too. It doesn't mean that he was."

"But, don't you see?" I say. "No one mentioned that Cat might be stolen until the senator brought it up. That shows that Senator Futzenburg might know something—something nobody else does."

Daphne's finger stops circling. "Maybe. Or maybe it just means that the senator is as suspicious as you are. Besides, what about that dog we just saw up near the fire tower? You don't think that was Cat?"

"Do you?" I counter.

She pauses, then shakes her head. "I guess not.

I didn't really get a great look at it, but that was a busy street. If it was Cat, somebody would have picked him up already."

"If they could catch him."

"Well, do *you* think it was Cat?" Daphne asks.

I also shake my head. "Probably not. That dog didn't really act lost."

"No."

"Which leads us back to Senator Futzenburg."

Right then, a high-school-age waitress brings us our shakes. We halt our conversation to dive into the thick, sweet, cold, heavenly, spectacular, scrumptious, chocolaty concoctions in front of us. I slurp up my shake so fast that a blizzard of pain howls through my head. The straw falls from my teeth.

"Brain freeze," I gasp.

"Me, too," Daphne moans, letting her head smack down onto the tabletop.

While my brain slowly thaws to normal temperature, my eyes roam around the Parrot.

Daphne and I discovered the Parrot the day after we arrived in Helena. We quickly realized that the candy and ice-cream parlor was hands-down Helena's best attraction—better than the Capitol, better than the History Museum, better than, well, anything. Apparently, it's been around forever. You can spend hours studying the Indian rugs hanging on the walls, the miniature elephant herd thundering along the display shelves and, of course, the toy parrots perched between the drop-down fluorescent lights. Besides the old-fashioned booths we're sitting in, the Parrot boasts a soda counter with round, rotating stools in front of it and a big mirror on the other side. Closer to the door, glass cases stuffed with homemade candy scream "Eat me! Eat me!"

For a kid with cash in his pockets, the Parrot is a very dangerous place.

I pull my eyes away from an old-fashioned juke-box sitting nearby, and ask, "So, what do you think?"

Daphne lifts her head back up off of the table and tucks her hair behind her ears. "About what?"

"Do you think Senator Futzenburg knows something about the governor's dog?"

Daphne takes another sip—a *smaller* sip—of her shake. "I doubt it. Why would he?"

"Well," I tell her. "He was talking about that special session the governor called. You know, it was on the front page today, along with the story about Cat and the story about the grizzly bears causing trouble up in Glacier Park."

"You didn't give me time to read *those*."

"I heard my mom and dad talking about it. They said there's not enough money set aside for schools this year. The governor called all the state lawmakers back to Helena to fix the problem."

"Oh, maybe I did hear about that," Daphne says.

"But what's that got to do with Cat?"

"Well," I say. "The senator seemed pretty mad about it."

Again, Daphne gives me her irritated frog look. "And just why would that make him steal Cat?"

I have to admit that I don't know.

We sit there for a moment nursing our shakes. Then another thought hits me. "Wait a minute. Maybe it doesn't have anything to do with the special session. Maybe it's more than that."

"And that would be...?"

"Well, who is Governor Rickson's biggest rival?"

"Probably Senator Futzenburg," Daphne answers. "Didn't he run against Governor Rickson in the last election?"

"You bet he did," I say, still remembering the sea of political yard signs covering Missoula. "And the vote was really close. Probably close enough for him to try again next time, right?"

"Maybe..." Daphne says.

"So think about it. How much is Cat worth to Governor Rickson's popularity?"

"Probably a lot."

"Not probably," I tell her. "Governor Rickson won the last election by only a couple of points. My mom said the 'dog vote' put him over the top. I mean, who doesn't trust someone who loves dogs?"

The last of Daphne's shake rattles up the straw

into her mouth. "Okay, I admit it. You might be on to something."

I sit up straighter. "I *am* on to something. If Cat was out of the way, it could pave the way for Senator Futzenburg to become our next governor!"

Several kids in another booth look over at us and snicker. Daphne pushes her empty shake glass to the side. "Even if it's true—which I doubt—I still don't see how that helps us."

I glance around to make sure no one is listening. Then, I lean forward and whisper, "We need more information. What if we go to the senator's office to see what we can find out?"

Daphne crosses her arms across her chest and leans back. Her skeptical greenish eyes bore into me. "If I had *anything* else to do, I'd say forget it."

"Buuuut…?"

She sighs dramatically. "When do you want to go?"

I grin. "How about—oh, shoot, what time is it?"

Daphne glances up at the wall clock. "Almost 1:00."

I leap out of the booth. "My science class!"

Eight

Daphne races with me down Last Chance Gulch, the chocolate milkshakes slopping around our guts like soggy soccer balls. At Lawrence Street—the one we live on—Daphne stops and peels left toward home.

"Bye," I shout to her without slowing down. "Come over later, okay?"

"'Kay," she calls back, dried chocolate milkshake still streaking her chin.

I continue down Last Chance Gulch until I come to the Great Northern Town Center.

The center is new, a tidy collection of shops, condos, a hotel and movie theater. At its far end stands a carousel and, next to it, a modern hands-on science center. I race into the science center and double-stair jump to the top floor.

My class is already in full swing.

"Sorry I'm late," I pant.

"It's cool," says Sebastian, a student instructor who acts like he'd rather be living in the Sixties than the present. "We're studying animal tracks today. Grab a seat at one of the tables."

When I said earlier that I was left to entertain myself all summer, that wasn't strictly true. Since we're in an actual city this summer instead of out in the middle of some wilderness, Mom and Dad signed me up for a science class that meets twice a week.

It's probably no surprise that I love science. It's in my blood. Dad's a geologist, of course, but Mom's a homegrown naturalist and an artist, too. She always sets up bird feeders and, in the summer, paints large canvasses of native plants in whatever biome we happen to be residing.

Anyway, in today's class we learn differences between footprints of Montana mammals. It's a lot of fun. I actually recognize most of them from hikes with Mom and Dad. The dainty prints of raccoons. The hand-sized paw print of a mountain lion. The unbelievably huge—and scary—meat hooks of the grizzly. During the last hour, we use real, preserved paws and hooves of animals to make plaster casts of tracks in sand. I want to do the grizzly, but some local kid beats me to it. I choose a moose instead.

The local kid smirks and says, "My grizzly's gonna eat your moose."

"Yeah?" I answer. "Well, my moose is full of deadly parasitic worms that are going to make your grizzly die a slow and painful death."

That shuts the boy up.

When I get home after class, Lily gallops down the short hallway and slams into my knees.

"SATE!" she yells, not quite mastering the 'L' in my name.

I scoop her up in my arms. "Did you poop on the potty today?"

"I saw a lion!" she exclaims.

Even I am surprised. "You did?"

"Yes. A dandy-lion!"

I laugh, putting her down. She follows me into the kitchen, where Mom and Dad sit relaxing with iced tea at the kitchen table.

"Hey, there he is," Dad greets me. "How was class?"

Dad is a little older than some of the other dads I know, but I probably wouldn't trade him in. He's forty-five and medium height, but wiry and strong from hauling a seventy-pound backpack during dozens of geology field seasons. Only a few gray worms peek out from his curly black hair.

"Class was good," I answer, my stomach grumbling.

"Did you get there on time?" Mom asks, still wearing a painting apron dotted with colorful spots.

"Yeees. Sort of." I say, but it's ironic that Mom is concerned about *my* schedule. While Dad is the King of Organization, Mom proudly refers to herself as "organizationally challenged"—which is obvious when I open the refrigerator. Every shelf is crammed with almost-empty cartons, bowls of leftovers, and half-full glasses of juice and milk.

"Dad's going to do BBQ pretty soon," Mom tells me.

"Whew," I mutter, relieved that I don't have to try to figure out which food is safe and which has turned into a Level 4 biohazard. I close the fridge and lean back against it. "What did you both do today?"

Mom smiles and says, "Thanks for asking! I spent the afternoon on a painting of peonies and lupines in the backyard, experimenting with some new color-mixing techniques."

Ah, I think, that explains Lily's 'dandy lions'. "What did you do, Dad?"

Dad reaches over and pulls my sister, squirming like a salamander, into his lap. "Unfortunately, not much. I was just telling your mom that Daphne's father and I hiked up an entire canyon looking for a good fault scarp to dig a trench."

My dad and Len—Daphne's father—work on a lot of different projects together, but lately, they've been especially interested in earthquake faults—places where pieces of the earth slip or move against each other. California gets more headlines for its earthquakes, but Montana is riddled with earthquake fault zones. That's not so surprising if you happen to notice the giant, jagged mountain ranges crisscrossing the western half of the state.

The reason we're spending the summer in Helena is because it was jolted by a series of three big earthquakes in 1935. The quakes toppled chimneys, demolished brand-new Helena High School, and killed four people. Dad and Len are checking to see which of the faults in the area might still be active. To do that, Dad locates good places to dig along the different fault lines. Then Len swoops in and dates the rock layers to find out how often each fault slips and causes an earthquake.

"Did you find any good places to dig?" I ask Dad.

"We're not sure. The canyon is pretty overgrown and we may have missed something. I think we're going to take a break from our search and drive up to east Glacier next week. Len wants to collect a couple of rock samples from a basalt dike for another study we're working on."

"Can me and Daphne go with you?" I ask. Glacier National Park is my favorite place in Montana—maybe in the whole world.

"I want to go to Glacier!" Lily shouts.

"Don't you have science class that day?" Mom asks me. "We didn't pay for that class just so you can skip it."

Dad waves a dismissive hand. "It's not a good trip for you to come anyway, Slate. We're going to leave before dawn, hike all day, and probably not get back until midnight."

"I don't mind," I said.

"Maybe next time," Dad tells me.

My shoulders slump. Then I warn him, "Watch out for the bears."

Dad smiles. "Yeah. I heard they were back in the news, bothering the terrified tourists."

"They had to close some campgrounds in the Many Glacier Valley," I say, repeating what I'd read in the morning newspaper.

"I was listening to Montana Public Radio today," Mom adds, "and they said they've brought up some Karelian bear dogs to use on the bears."

"Really?" I've never heard of a Karelian bear dog, but they sound cool.

"Yes," Mom explains. "These dogs were originally trained as hunting dogs in Europe or Russia or somewhere like that. Supposedly, they are fearless around bears, barking and nipping at them. Biologists have been using them to teach the bears to stay away from people."

"Well, let's hope it works," Dad says. "You know what they say—a fearless bear is a dead bear. If a grizzly becomes too much of a problem, the rangers have no choice but to kill it."

"That stinks," I say. "It's not the bears' faults we invade their territories."

Mom is about to say something more when Daphne calls through the screen door. "Hello? Anyone home?"

Nine

At the sound of Daphne's voice, a feeling like a wet fish starts thrashing around inside my chest cavity. I wish it wouldn't keep doing that, but it can't seem to help itself lately. I have a sneaking suspicion what the problem is, and it's getting very annoying.

"Back here!" Mom yells.

A moment later, Daphne walks into the kitchen. "Hi Dr. and Mrs. Stephens."

"Daphne, you know you can call us Andrew and Sarah."

Daphne smiles and shrugs. "Old habit."

"So what are you up to?" my mother asks.

"I just came over to talk to Slate about the governor's dog. He probably told you that we spent the morning looking for him."

My parents throw surprised glances my way. "No," Mom says. "He didn't happen to mention that little item. Did you find him?"

"I saw a dog!" Lily proudly exclaims.

Daphne steps over and rubs my sister's head of wispy brown hair. A dozen strands stick straight up like floating tentacles of a sea anemone. "I'll bet you did, Lily!" Daphne tells her. "Was it a big one?"

My sister's eyes grow wide and she nods. "It was the *biggest*."

We all crack up. No doubt about it. Three-year-olds make the best comedians.

Daphne straightens up and answers my mother's question. "We followed one dog that might have been Cat, but we lost him before we could be sure. We're not ready to give up."

"You want to go to my room?" I ask, eager for some privacy.

"I want to come!" Lily says.

"Mo-om," I plead.

"You have to stay here sweetheart."

Dad tickles Lily before she can object, and Daphne and I make a quick getaway.

"So," I ask Daphne, as we climb the stairs. "Did you think any more about my idea?"

"You mean talking to Senator Futzenburg?"

"Well, I wasn't thinking of *talking* to him."

We reach my room and Daphne deposits herself in the chair at my desk. "You mean you want to spy on him?"

I sit on the floor and lean back against my bed. "I wouldn't call it spying. Maybe just, uh, *reconnoitering*."

"Yeah. Spying," she says, unfazed by the word. "Anyway, if we're going to wander all over town, don't you think it would be smarter to go back to where we saw that dog today and look for him?"

"We can do that, too," I said, "but we both agreed that probably wasn't Cat. And besides, I've just got a feeling Senator Futzenburg knows something. Are you in?"

"Well, I'll have to look at my busy appointments calendar. Oh, and I need to paint my toenails in the morning."

"It won't make your toes smell any better," I say.

Daphne picks up an eraser from my desk and fires it at me. Thanks to my superhuman fast reflexes, it only grazes my ear.

"Is that an answer?" I ask.

"On one condition. I get to veto any of your dumb ideas."

I snort, insulted. "My ideas are *never* dumb."

"Agree or go by yourself."

I growl. "Okay."

The next morning, Daphne and I head back to the Capitol. The first-floor security guard still clutches the paperback copy of *Total Destruction* he was reading yesterday.

"Is everything destroyed yet?" I ask him.

The guard lifts his head, and stares at me blankly. I point. "In the book."

"Oh," he answers. "Not yet."

"We're looking for Senator Futzenburg's office," Daphne tells him.

More blank look, and I'm beginning to think the

man's brain has gone elk hunting and left his body behind. But it's not that after all.

"Well," the guard says, studying a map in front of him. "To be honest, I'm not sure where his office is. You know that the legislators don't keep regular offices here."

"You mean because they don't meet every year?" Daphne asks.

"Right."

For those of you who aren't lucky enough to live in Montana, I guess I should explain that last statement. If you're from New York or Florida—maybe even Nebraska—your state legislature probably meets every year.

That's not the case in Montana.

We're one of the only states in the country where the senate and house of representatives meet only every *other* year.

I know what you're going to ask next, and the answer is I don't know why the legislature doesn't meet more often. I'm guessing that running the state interferes with hunting, camping, bull-riding, and other more vital activities.

"So," Daphne says to the guard. "You're saying that Senator Futzenburg doesn't have an office here?"

The guard rubs his chin. "Well, since he's the Minority Leader, he probably does have an office somewhere. I've just never heard of it. Check up on the third floor. There's a lot of temporary offices that the senators and representatives can use up there. I'm not sure who's using what right now.

"Here," he says, handing us a little map of the Capitol's floor plans. "Maybe this will help."

Armed with the floor-plan map, Daphne and I ride the elevator up to the third floor. We emerge next to a full-size bronze sculpture of one of Montana's most famous statesmen, U.S. Senator Mike Mansfield, and his wife Maureen.

Daphne has again brought her camera and takes a quick picture of me hamming it up with the Mansfields. Then she asks, "Which way?"—to me, that is, not Senator Mansfield and his wife.

We walk a few steps to a long hallway. To our right—east, I calculate—the hallway looks fairly deserted. To the left, we see more than a dozen people walking or talking in small groups.

"This way," I say, moving toward the people.

"Even if we find the senator, what are we going to say?" Daphne whispers.

"I don't know," I whisper back. "Let's just play it by ear."

Daphne hates those kinds of answers. She's always the GWTP—the Girl With The Plan. I've discovered, though, that sometimes you just gotta wing it. Besides, Daphne is usually so confident, it's worth being vague about things just to see her squirm.

As we reach the end of the hallway, we see a sign to our left that reads "Senate Chamber." A boy a little older than I am suddenly hurries out the door, allowing us a glimpse of an enormous room inside. It looks almost exactly like that giant room where the President of the United States gives his State of the Union speeches on television every year. Several senators sit up on raised seats at the far end of the room, facing their colleagues who are all assembled at fancy wooden desks arranged in concentric semi-circles. Before the door swings closed again, we actually see Senator Futzenburg, red-faced, shouting at his fellow senators about something.

"It looks like they're in session," Daphne says. "We'd better come back later."

"Are you kidding?" I whisper. "This is perfect timing. C'mon, let's find his office."

We hurry onward, through a lobby packed with people standing around talking, guzzling soft drinks, and eating snacks. The same kid we just saw is now hurrying back toward us, and I stop him. His hair is neatly combed and he's probably the only boy in Montana wearing a suit.

"Do you work here?" I ask him.

He stands straighter and lifts his nose, as if offended that I even ask. "I'm one of the pages," he says.

"Is that like an errand boy or something?" I needle him.

His cheeks flush. *"No.* I pass messages to the senators and get them things."

Like I said, an errand boy. But instead of insulting him further, I ask. "Do you know where Senator Futzenburg's office is?"

"Well, it's not around here," he says. "Check the fourth floor."

He dashes away, and Daphne and I continue on through the lobby room.

Daphne looks at our map. "Fourth floor?" she says. "It doesn't even *show* a fourth floor."

I point. "Look, there's some stairs."

We push through a door into a narrow stairwell, and climb up to the Capitol's top floor. Soon, we are astonished to find ourselves in a balcony, looking down on a second huge chamber. The chamber is similar to the Senate Chamber, but has twice as many people sitting in it.

Daphne consults the map that the guard gave us. "This must be the House of Representatives Chamber," she whispers.

"Yeah. C'mon, let's keep looking."

Ten

We leave the House of Representatives Chamber and hurry back toward the other end of the Capitol. Beyond the rotunda, the fourth floor seems as if space aliens have just vacuumed up everybody to turn them into plant fertilizer or something.

"This is creepy," Daphne says. "Where is everyone?"

"I guess they're all downstairs," I tell her. "Let's go back to the third floor."

We descend another narrow stairwell and walk through a short corridor. On one side of us are offices and on the other, a large room labeled Law Library on our map. We circle all the way around the library until we come to a row of cubicles fitted against the east wall of the Capitol. We hear voices behind two of them and smell coffee.

"Would the Minority Leader set up here?" Daphne whispers.

"I don't think so," I say slowly. "He's too important to settle for a cubicle, isn't he?"

I am just about to give up, when Daphne and I push through one last door into a claustrophobic, dimly-lit hallway.

"Score!" I say.

On a door right in front of us, gold lettering spells the words, "Senate Minority Leader".

"This is it!"

"Okay, but now what?" asks Daphne.

I glance in both directions and press my ear to the glass.

"I don't hear anyone."

"Slate, we are *not* going in there. Remember what I said about vetoing your dumb ideas?"

Before she can object further, I grab her arm and turn the knob to the door. Like most doors in Montana, it is unlocked.

"Slate!" Daphne hisses, but we are already in.

I quickly close the door behind us.

"Slate, this is crazy!"

"Shhh!" I tell her, looking around the large room.

The office is actually a lot nicer than I would have guessed—especially considering it's almost impossible to find it without a GPS locator, a pack of bloodhounds, and an aboriginal tracker or two. An enormous wooden desk fills one end of the room, framed by floor-to-ceiling bookshelves. A couch sits under the north-facing windows, and Native American and Western art hangs from walls or sits on shelves, along with photos of the senator with other famous people.

"Is that President Nixon?" I ask, stepping over to examine one old photo.

"*Slate!*" Daphne hisses. "*What are we doing here?*"

"Oh, right," I say, pulling my attention from the photo. "Look for clues."

"What kind of clues?" Daphne demands.

"Anything to do with Cat."

I step over to the senator's gigantic wooden desk. Papers are scattered all across it. Most have numbers such as "SB 483" on top of them, followed by language that looks like it was invented by robots using a random word choice function. Stuff like "On this day of 2011, it is hereby resolved by unanimous octopuses that peritoneal plutocrats convey an acceptance of the promulgations by the senator from Mineral County that..."

You get the idea.

While I look over the desk, Daphne studies the floor-to-ceiling bookcases behind it.

"Slate," she whispers, her eyes scanning the shelves. "I don't like *being* in here. That elk probably has a security camera in it."

I glance up to see a big deer head looking down at us from the far wall.

"I doubt it," I tell her. "They never hide security cameras in elk. Moose and grizzly bears, maybe, but elk. Forget it."

Daphne is not amused.

"Even if Senator Futzenburg knows something, why would he leave evidence in here? I mean, do you think he'd have dog dishes full of food and water sitting on top of his desk?"

"No, but...wait!"

My roving eyes suddenly stop at a sticky note attached to the corner of the senator's desk. On the note are two words: Rickson Dog.

"Daphne, I think I've found something!"

She swivels around and takes a step. "What?"

And that's when we hear voices coming down the hallway.

Eleven

"The senator!" Daphne hisses.

Indeed, Senator Futzenburg's husky, down-home voice reverberates clearly through the glass-and-wooden door. It sounds as though he's talking to a woman, maybe his secretary or chief of staff.

Like a falcon's talons, Daphne's fingers dig into my forearm. "What are we going to *do*?"

I look all around the office. At least in Montana, old buildings like this almost never have closets, and the Capitol is no exception. That leaves us with only one possible place to hide. Quickly, I pull out the senator's chair and shove Daphne under his desk. I crawl into the space after her and ease the chair back in behind us.

"Slate, this is the stupidest—"

Before Daphne can finish her sentence, the office door creaks open and heavy footsteps clomp in.

"All we can do," we hear Senator Futzenburg telling the Unknown Female Person, "is to try to head this thing off at the pass. Call Senators Loveland and Petuniak. See if they'll meet me for coffee, say, about two o'clock?"

"Do you want to include Bonnie O'Reilly in the

meeting?" the UFP asks.

A pause. Then, the senator says, "Yep. Good idea. People seem to listen to her—the voice of reason, as my Daddy used to say."

"Will that be all?"

"Yep. Thanks, Liz. Hold my calls."

We hear the office door close and the Senator's heavy footsteps clomp over to a coat rack. After a pause, the footsteps walk toward the desk. *Toward us.*

"Gol-darn governor," Senator Futzenburg grumbles, talking to himself. "If you're going to call a special session, at least don't do it during fly fishin' season."

We can hear the senator breathing, and he begins tapping something—maybe a pen—on the desktop right above our heads.

Daphne clutches my forearm tighter.

My nerves are also jangling, but I realize I've got an even bigger problem than the senator.

Daphne.

In our cramped cave under the desk, we are squeezed so close together, that my nose is shoved up against her dark, thick hair. Her hair is soft, freshly-washed, and the smell of peach shampoo overpowers my senses. My heart starts pounding. My mind drifts. Before I can stop myself, I pucker up and kiss...

Her ear.

Her response is immediate.

"What are you DOING?"

Daphne scrambles out from beneath the desk with me close behind. As soon as she stands up, she whirls on me. "Slate, you slobbered on my ear!"

My head is still spinning from Daphne's peach-scented shampoo, and the only response I can spit out is, "I...I did not!"

"You did, too." Daphne wipes her ear. "Oh yuck!"

That's when a loud voice booms, "EXCUSE ME!"

We both snap our heads toward Senator Futzenburg, who towers above us looking as though he's just been shot out of a cannon right into the middle of a circus.

"Who in the blazes are you and where did you come from?" he demands.

The ear incident had made me forget all about Senator Futzenburg, but now the gravity of our situation slams down like a bale of hay.

"Uh..."

"How did you kids get in here?" the senator demands, his face a familiar shade of red.

"We got lost?" I toss out.

"Liz!" the senator bellows, and a moment later, a middle-aged woman in a business suit—the Unknown Female Person herself—bursts through the door. "What is it?" she asks, clearly alarmed.

"Call Security."

Daphne throws out both hands as if she's halting traffic. "No, wait!"

Liz and Senator Futzenburg stare at her.

"We're sorry for sneaking in," Daphne says. "We only came because of Cat."

"Daphne!" I say. Hasn't she ever heard of a convenient little thing called *lying*???

The senator looks confused and glances around his office. "Cat? What cat? I don't see any gol-darned cat in here!"

"Not *a* cat. You know, Cat, the governor's dog."

"Ugh!" I say, slapping my forehead.

But understanding begins to dawn on the senator's face, and his jaw muscles relax a notch. He grumbles, "Oh *that* Cat. As if I don't have enough problems."

"Do you still want me to call Security?" Liz asks.

Senator Futzenburg waves his hand. "Naw. I think I can handle this."

Liz leaves and the senator points to the blue couch under the window. We go sit down while he steps around his desk. "So," he says, settling into his chair. "Let's hear about the governor's gol-darned dog."

Daphne and I look at each other, each hoping the other will start first. Finally, Daphne says, "We're worried about him."

"Yeah," I add in a dazzling display of oratory.

"When we saw the headlines yesterday," Daphne continues. "We decided to see if we could help find him."

The senator huffs and says, "I guess I buy it so far. But what's that go to do with me?"

Daphne casts accusing hazel eyes in my direction.

"*What?*" I ask.

"Tell him."

I sigh. "Well," I begin. "We heard you talking outside the Parrot yesterday. I just thought…"

"Thought what?" Senator Futzenburg insists.

"Well, I just thought that you might know something."

Another dawning spreads across the senator's face, and suddenly he lets loose with a guffaw. The guffaw quickly turns to chuckles. Then it escalates into some of the loudest belly laughs I've ever heard. The senator tries to talk, but the laughs engulf his words. He slaps his knees and then begins choking. He rises out of his chair and staggers over to open his office door.

"Liz!" he croaks. "Water!"

A moment later, Liz hurries in and hands him a glass, and the senator guzzles half of it. Then, he clomps back over and plants his behind on the edge of his desk, facing toward us.

"So you kids figured I snuffed out Governor Rickson's dog?"

I am embarrassed by this time, but not quite enough to abandon my theory. "Yeah," I say. "Did you?"

Another aftershock of chortles ripples through

the senator. He tells us, "I only wish I'd thought of it! As my Daddy would say, that dog's been a royal pain in my patootee."

"See?" Daphne says to me. "I told you it was a stupid idea."

The senator plucks at one of his bushy eyebrows. "Believe me, I've seen worse things in politics. When it comes to elections, almost anything's fair game. But no, if I'm ever going to beat the governor, I'll have to do it fair and square."

"But what about that sticky note?" I persist.

The senator glances behind him. "What sticky— oh, that. Look, kids. I don't have the memory of you youngsters. As you can see, I need to remind myself about all kinds of things."

I look at his desk more closely and see that, indeed, it is tiled with sticky notes from east to west.

"I probably scribbled that note after the press conference at the Parrot. Just a reminder to think of a better answer the next time some reporter decides to ask me about it."

"So, you don't think anyone stole Cat?" Daphne asks.

Senator Futzenburg takes another sip of water. Then, he shakes his head. "No. Not unless Governor Rickson stole him himself."

"Huh?"

"Well, think about it," the senator says with a sly grin. "What better way to get sympathy for something—in this case, that special session he's dragged us all into? Maybe he figured if he stole his own dog, it might distract good Montana citizens from the fact that this *ed-u-ca-tion* session is costing a heap of taxpayer dollars?"

"You really think he would have done that?" I ask.

The senator shrugs. "Go ask him."

Twelve

We thank Senator Futzenburg—for his help or for not sending us to jail, I'm not sure which.

"Don't mention it," he tells us. "Just do me a favor. Knock next time. And find that gol' darned dog. I got enough to worry about without Cat gobblin' up the headlines."

Liz gives us a couple of campaign buttons before we go. As we make our way back toward the stairwell, we actually decide to take the senator's advice and see if the governor is in. It's a longshot, but again, Montana is that kind of state. No one is so famous he won't ever talk to a regular citizen—especially one who might grow up to vote for him. We don't want to ask the governor if he stole his own dog, of course. That seems pretty, ahem, far-fetched. I do have a couple of other questions for him, though.

Of course, you're probably not thinking about that, are you? You're probably still wondering why I kissed Daphne on the ear. As we clomp down the stairs, I'm wondering about it myself. Here's the thing…

Daphne and I have known each other since we

were in the first grade. Her dad joined the U of M Geology Department only a year after my father did. Our families both bought houses in the University District, less than a mile from campus, and Daphne and I started attending all of the same schools. In school, we were usually in different classes and pretty much ignored each other. Outside of school, we sometimes went ice-skating at the fairgrounds or rode bikes together—if no one else was around.

But all of that changed at the end of third grade. That's when our fathers decided to start spending their summer field seasons together. When that happened, Daphne and I got to know each other better—a lot better. Daphne is an only child and Lily didn't come along until later, so Daphne and I were forced to spend all day, every day, hanging out together.

Not that it was so bad. Daphne's too stubborn and she *thinks* I'm too impulsive (I'm not, by the way), but we always got along pretty well. Sure, we fought three or four times a day, but we also had adventures together, read books together, ate together. It was almost like getting a new sister in a lot of ways. Yeah, that's what Daphne was like. A sister.

Which is why I'm so confused now.

This past year in sixth grade at Discovery Middle School, I started getting these weird thoughts and feelings about Daphne. I'd be walking through the halls between classes and see her standing next to the lockers with a group of friends. She'd tuck a strand of black hair behind her ear and burst into laughter about something. Sometimes, she'd see me and give a little wave and smile. That was the worst—the smile.

When that happened, my heart would just start popping like bacon in a frying pan. My skin sizzled and my arms and legs trembled. I'd stop talking in the middle of a sentence or stumble over my own feet.

"What's wrong?" my friends Ryan and Nick would ask me.

"Uh, nothing," I'd say. After all, what could I tell them? We'd all liked girls before but this...this was just too weird.

I had hoped that once the summer started, my strange new illness would cure itself and things would get back to normal. Instead, it's only gotten worse. Until now, I think I've done a pretty good job hiding it from Daphne. But then I had to go and kiss her. And on the ear! How could I be so dumb?

Daphne has to take some of the blame, too. As Senator Futzenburg might say, Daphne's gotten so "gol' darn pretty" lately. And what's with all that flirting and being so charming? In fact, as we approach the Governor's Office, I can see her getting ready to do it all again...

"Hello again," Daphne gushes, as we reach the receptionist.

The man looks up at us, blank for a moment. Then his face breaks into a smile. "Oh, it's you."

Oh it's you, I think sourly. Who else would it be, you pile of dried deer droppings?

"What are you up to today?" the man asks us.

Daphne runs her hand through her hair and bats her eyes again. She really does, I swear! Makes me want to launch my breakfast.

"Well, I know this is probably impossible," she tells the man, "but..."

Daphne pauses, suddenly acting all shy or something.

Right, I think. *She's about as shy as a trapeze artist.*

"It's alright," the man encourages her. "What do you need?"

"Well," says Daphne. "We were wondering if it was *possible* we might talk to Governor Rickson— just for a minute or two."

To my astonishment, the man stands up. "Wait here. I'll go ask him."

Daphne and I turn to each other, jaws hanging. I even forget to be mad at Daphne as the man disappears. A moment later, the receptionist returns.

"Right this way," he says, sweeping an arm toward a short hallway.

Ahead, in a doorway, we suddenly see the sturdy bulk of Governor Rickson. He's wearing jeans and an open-necked shirt with a bolo tie. He smiles and extends a hand toward me.

"Hello," he says. "And who might you be?"

With my hand in his warm paw, I cannot utter a word.

Then, I croak, "Slate. Slate Stephens."

"Nice to meet you, Slate."

The governor releases my hand and grasps Daphne's. "And you, young lady?"

"Daphne McSweeney."

"McSweeney..." the governor muses. "Sounds like a good Montana Irish name to me."

"It-it is." I note with satisfaction that Daphne is too star-struck to put on her usual show of flirting.

"Come on in," the governor tells us. "I don't have long, but we've got a couple of minutes to chat."

We enter his office—which is a lot nicer and more comfortable than that of Senator Futzenburg—and sit down on a green leather couch next to a coffee table. The governor plops down in a chair at right angles to us.

"So," he asks, crossing one leg over another as if we're just sitting down for lemonade on his back porch. "Where are you both from?"

"Missoula," I say.

Daphne gives the governor a more complete account. "Our fathers are in the Geology Department at U of M," she tells him. "They're mapping the earthquake faults in the area, so we're here most of the summer."

The governor opens his eyes wide in mock concern. "We're not about to have a major earthquake, are we?"

"Probably not," I tell him.

He sits back, relieved. "Well, I hope not. I don't think the state budget can handle it this year."

Daphne and I both chuckle politely.

"So," says the governor. "What's on your minds?"

Thirteen

"**W**ell, sir," I say. "I don't know if your, um, *assistant* told you, but we're trying to help find Cat."

At Cat's name, the governor's face sags and his eyes water up. Either he's really worried about his dog, or he's the best actor on the planet.

"Oh, yes," he says, shaking his head. "I just don't know what happened. One minute he was with me. The next minute, he was gone, just like that. The more time goes by, the more I fear the worst."

"That's why we want to help."

Daphne pulls out the map of Helena with the governor's walking route traced on it. "Governor Rickson, yesterday we walked all along your regular walking route. But we found out that you don't always go the same way."

"Maybe," I take over, "you could tell us exactly where you went the morning Cat went missing?"

The governor nods and pulls out a pair of reading glasses and a pen from his shirt pocket. He sits forward and we all lean in over the map.

"You know," he says, "I've retraced that route in my head ever since Cat got lost. See here? I didn't actually take Broadway. I walked down this other street."

"That's what we guessed," Daphne says.

"Then, I stopped for my usual cuppa joe at The General Mercantile right here," he continues, putting an 'X' at a place on Last Chance Gulch.

"But Cat was still with you then, right?" I ask.

The governor nods, then chuckles. "Yep. Cat never wants to leave that place."

"Why not?" I ask. "Doesn't he want to keep walking?"

"Sure, but he's the biggest garbage hound in the capital. A lot of folks at the Merc are regulars like I am, and they sneak him all kinds of pastries. I ask them not to, but Cat's stomach is a bottomless pit. He'll eat until he throws up."

"But you left there with him?" Daphne asks.

The governor taps the pen a couple of times on the map and nods. "In fact, we didn't stay as long as usual, because I wanted to talk to my aides before the special session started up here. You've heard about the special session?"

"I read about it in the newspaper," I tell him.

Governor Rickson sits up straighter. "You know, a lot of people think I'm wasting money calling this session, but I couldn't let a whole year go by without doing something about this funding shortfall. Schools have been underfunded for decades in this state and it's a disgrace.

"I mean," the governor continues, building up steam, "I just can't abide people who say they don't want to pay for educating today's youth. They say things like 'My kids are grown. Why should I have to pay for other people's kids to go to school?' That is not the kind of selfish attitude that made this country great! Do I have to remind them that someone else paid for *their* kids to go to school?"

The governor's face has flushed red by this time, and I can tell he really believes in what he's saying. Then, he catches himself and smiles. "Sorry kids. I didn't mean to give you a speech. I guess we politicians just can't help ourselves sometimes."

We again chuckle politely.

"So where were we?" the governor asks, returning his attention to the map.

"The coffee shop," I tell him. "You said Cat left there with you."

"When did you first notice that he was missing?" Daphne asks.

The governor studies the map for another moment. Then, he jabs the pen down. "Right about here."

I look. The pen is sticking into an intersection near the Cathederal of St. Helena.

"Are you sure that's where he went missing?"

Governor Rickson sighs. "No. No, I'm afraid not. My mind was on other things. Usually, I don't have to think too much about Cat. He just keeps up with me. To be honest, he could have wandered off several blocks before here. I just don't know."

I can read the guilt etched across the governor's face, and it makes me feel sorry for him.

All three of us sit quietly for a moment. Then, Daphne asks, "Is there anything else you can tell us about Cat?"

The governor lets out a big sigh. "As you know, he was really friendly with almost everyone. I suppose he could have gotten into a car with a stranger, but..."

"But what?"

"I just don't think he'd do that. To be honest, I'm completely flummoxed."

I've never heard the word, but it's not hard to figure out what it means. Daphne and I stand up.

"Thank you for taking time to talk to us," Daphne says.

"Anything I can do to help," the governor says, putting his hand over his chest. "It means a lot to me to know you and other people are out looking for him. In many ways, Cat is—was—my best friend."

Daphne asks the governor if he'd mind if she took a couple of pictures of him and me together.

"I've got a better idea," the governor says and calls for the smarmy receptionist to come in. "Can you get a couple of snapshots of us all together?"

"Sure," the guy says.

At the governor's prompt, we all say "re-e-lec-tion" and the camera clicks. We're about to step out of the office, when I think of one more question.

"Governor?" I ask.

He looks down at me. "Yes?"

"Maybe we missed this in the news, but Cat was wearing a collar, wasn't he?"

The governor's face darkens. He sighs and shakes his head. "No, he wasn't. I know. I know. I should have had one on him, but Border collies have sensitive skin and Cat's collar gives him a rash. Besides, he's just never wandered away like this."

"We understand," Daphne tells him. "If I were Cat, I wouldn't want to wear a collar, either."

"Don't worry," I add. "If we don't find him, somebody will."

The governor forces a smile, and I can tell he doesn't believe me.

I'm not sure I believe me either.

Fourteen

Despite our excitement at the Capitol, neither Daphne nor I say a word as we ride the trolley back downtown. I tell myself that maybe Daphne is tired, or is thinking about our meetings with Governor Rickson and Senator Futzenburg. But I know that's not it. She and I are thinking about the same thing—the Ear Kiss.

I wonder if I should say something. You know, make up some lame excuse or deny it happened all together? But I'm pretty sure that will only make things worse.

Finally, Daphne clears her throat. She turns her head so that her hazel eyes bore into me.

"Slate," she says.

I swallow. "Yeah?"

Oh boy, here it comes now. Our friendship is over. That's it. Forever.

"Slate," she says again, and my heart starts fibrillating like one of those massage machines they build into easy chairs.

"Slate," she says.

"*What?*"

"I'm hungry."

I choke back a gasp of relief and swallow.

"Yeah," I tell her. "Me too. Where do you want to go?"

"Well." She pauses. "I was thinking. Now that we know where Cat disappeared, we can focus our search more."

"You mean between the Mercantile and St. Helena's Cathedral?"

She nods. "If someone took Cat, that's where it happened."

I flinch in surprise. "Wait a minute. I thought you said it was a dumb idea that Cat could have been kidnapped. You mean you've changed your mind?"

"Well," she backpedals, "I'm still sure there are better explanations, but..."

"But you don't think I'm crazy after all."

Her face flushes and suddenly, I want to kiss her again.

Stop that! I command my brain. *What is WRONG with you?*

"You *are* crazy," she says, "but I can't think of a better explanation at the moment."

I grin in triumph. "Maybe we should also talk to some people down there. See if they saw anything."

"Maybe."

"But that still doesn't answer where you want to eat."

We decide to grab burritos at a place called Taco del Sol, close to the Parrot. Afterward, I pick pinto beans out of my braces while we cruise down Last

Chance Gulch to the General Mercantile.

Neither of us have been to the Merc before, and it feels like entering a dark cave, especially after the bright sunlight outside. As our eyes adjust, I see that it's actually more like a mine shaft than a cave. A mine shaft that smells like coffee. To our right is a coffee bar with round stools similar to the Parrot. On the left, are displays of candles and other gifts, hilarious greeting cards, and sticky notes with funny phrases, some of them too rude to repeat. Best of all, the whole place is done up in rough wood beams and paneling so that you really can imagine you've been transported back a hundred years into Helena's frontier past.

That illusion vanishes as we walk farther back into the mine shaft, er, I mean store. There, we encounter a wide mix of students, workers, and business people sitting around rough-cut tables sipping coffee, chatting, texting, and working on laptop computers.

"I can see why Governor Rickson likes this place," I tell Daphne.

Suddenly, a tall, friendly fellow wearing an old-time vest and cowboy boots approaches us. "Hello. I'm Jack. Can I help you two?"

Daphne takes over, and I begin to wonder if she only does that when we meet a *man*.

"Hi," she says, but without quite the flirty voice she used with the governor's receptionist. "I'm

Daphne and this is Slate. We're trying to help find the governor's dog."

The man slowly combs his fingers through his thinning hair. He drops his eyes and makes a sad little "Mm-mm" sound. "We're just devastated about that. You know that Cat was a regular here?"

"The governor told us," I say.

"None of us can figure out what could have happened to him," Jack continues. "In fact, he and the governor stopped by the morning Cat went missing."

"That's what we heard."

Jack raises his eyes back up. "What is it I can help you with?"

"We're sure the police have already been by," Daphne says, "but we just wondered if anyone here might have seen anything after the governor and Cat left?"

"I don't know," Jack says, "but let's go ahead and ask."

Before I can object, Jack turns around and announces, "Hey, listen up everyone!"

The din of conversation drips to a halt. All eyes turn toward us, and Daphne and I glance nervously at each other.

"These two fine citizens," Jack begins, placing hands on each of our shoulders, "are trying to help find Cat."

Approving murmurs fill the air and I see people nodding their heads.

"All of us here have a special place in our hearts

for Cat, and these kids are wondering if anyone saw anything noteworthy two days ago, the morning Cat disappeared?"

Again, murmuring. I see a couple of people exchange words and others shake their heads. Then, one fellow speaks out.

"You know, I did see one woman come in here that morning, just after the governor and Cat left. Don't know if it means anything, but I'd never noticed her before."

"I remember her," a woman in another booth pipes in. "She was about my age."

"We'd *all* remember another hundred year-old gal," the man across from her jokes. Everyone laughs.

The woman makes as if to throw her coffee on him. Then, she adds, "She was wearing a red jacket with some kind of silhouette on it."

"Oh yeah," another man joins in. "It was an animal. A wolf maybe."

"That's right," the woman says. "A wolf."

A pause fills the room.

"Anyone else?" Jack asks. "Anyone see where this woman went?"

The first man says, "Don't know, but she didn't stay long. Just filled up her travel mug and left."

"Okay, thanks."

Jack returns his attention to us. "Well, I doubt that was any help."

"You never know," Daphne says, "it might be.

Thank you for your time."

"Yeah, thanks," I add.

We start to turn back toward the front entrance, but Jack says, "Hey, why don't you cut out through the back? It's kind of neat, and that's the way the governor and Cat often leave. Oh, and you look like you could use some supplies. How about a couple of scones for the road?"

Daphne and I look at each other.

"Sure!" we say together.

Jack walks around behind the counter and hands us each a chocolate chip scone.

"Let us know if there's anything else we can do," he tells us as we leave. "It'll break my heart if that dog doesn't turn up safe."

Fifteen

After pushing through the back door of the Merc, we walk through a cool little underground brick passageway and climb a short flight of concrete stairs. We find ourselves up on Jackson Street, a street that runs parallel to Last Chance Gulch.

"To the cathedral?" I ask, taking a bite of the chocolate chip scone.

Daphne nods, also munching away. "Keep your eyes open."

As if she has to tell *me*. Typical girl, trying to take credit for everything.

To reach the cathedral we have to walk south one block and then turn left and walk several more blocks. We walk slowly, and I ratchet up my attention, scanning the ground for every detail. The problem, of course, is that concrete doesn't hold dog tracks—or any other kind of tracks—very well. Still, I sharpen my focus and try to look for any dog sign I can find. At the intersection, we're about to turn left toward the cathedral, when Daphne swallows her last bite of scone and says, "Hey, can we take a minute and go up to the bookstore? I finished Book Six in the *Vampires in Hollyweird* series."

"Finished it? Didn't you get that, like, three days ago?"

"Two," she said. "I stayed up late to read it last night."

I'm thinking that she probably stayed up late hoping to *meet* a vampire to fall in love with, but I'm on shaky ground after the Ear Kiss, so I don't say anything.

I shrug. "Okay."

Instead of turning left, we continue straight, up Jackson. We walk about fifty feet, when my shoes skid to a halt.

"What is it?" Daphne asks.

Next to the sidewalk, some low shrubs are growing, and I reach down toward one. I pluck something off of the shrub and straighten up.

"Look," I say, offering my pinched fingers to Daphne.

She takes what I give her and studies it for a moment. Then, her surprised eyes meet mine.

"Hair," she says.

"Dog hair. Do you still have that photo of Cat?"

Daphne pulls it out of her pocket and we stand close together, looking at it. Daphne's fruity scent again fills my nostrils and I have to fight off the dizziness swimming through my brain.

"The hair is the right color," Daphne says. "Black and white."

"Yeah…" I say, glancing at the fur, "but something's

not right about it. This hair is straight. Look, Cat's hair is more wavy or curly."

"I suppose it could have straightened up in this weather," Daphne says.

"Wouldn't it have gotten curlier as it dried out?"

"Hm. You're probably right."

We both start picking through the shrubs and find more black and white hair, but all of it is straight. Daphne takes a couple of photos with her camera, just in case we might need them later. Then I step into another clue.

"Ew, what's that smell?" Daphne asks, straightening up.

I look down to see my right foot firmly planted in a large olive-colored, slightly encrusted, much-too-soft pile of dog poop.

"Crap," I say.

Daphne bursts out laughing. "That's what it is, all right."

I start impatiently scraping my shoe off on the edge of the curb.

"Slate, that's *gross!*"

"Well what do you suggest, All-Knowing One?"

She spreads her hands, palms up. "You stepped in it, you figure it out. You'd just better stay here while I go inside the store."

Daphne disappears inside a store called The Montana Book and Toy Company. By the time she emerges, I've gotten as much of the poop off of my shoe as I'm going to. I just hope that what's left, stuck inside my treads, doesn't dry too much before I can find a hose to squirt it out.

"Did you get your book?" I ask.

"No!" Daphne gruffs. "Some stupid girl bought the last copy this morning."

Just to see Daphne's reaction, I ask, "Couldn't you skip ahead and read Book 8?"

Daphne shoots me a dirty scowl, and her voice oozes with sarcasm. "Oh *sure*! Maybe I could just watch the movie when it comes out, too!"

With this kind of reaction, I can't resist pressing ahead.

"I don't see what's so special about vampires anyway," I tell her. "Mosquitoes drink more blood every second than all the vampires in the whole history of the world—unless you're talking about real vampire bats, that is."

Daphne lets out an incredulous "Uh!" that sounds like the hiss of pressure from a steam locomotive. "Slate, don't you know anything? The books are not about vampires!"

"They aren't? But the title says—"

"I mean they are, but they aren't! They're about love and beauty and courage—"

"And vampires."

Another steam locomotive sound.

"Boys don't understand," Daphne says. "The books are too sophisticated for the male mind."

"You're right," I tell her. "It's *way* too sophisticated to believe in creatures that don't exist and then pretend that they're more interesting than the real world."

Daphne clenches her hands into fists. "Argh! Let's just keep looking for Cat before we have to stop being friends," she tells me, stomping back toward the stop sign.

I walk after her, suppressing a grin. My victory has been secured. Besides riling her up to record levels, I've also gotten her to admit that we're still friends. Which is a relief, despite her recent attempts to flirt with every Y chromosome she happens to meet.

Back at the stop sign, we turn right and walk all the way up to the cathedral, one of Helena's most visible landmarks. According to the guidebook I read, the cathedral was built by the town's huge Catholic community—the same worshippers who built Carroll College across town. I've never been to Europe, but the cathedral looks like it could easily fit in there, with its Gothic arches and soaring spires. Come to think of it, one of Daphne's vampires could probably live in it, too.

"What do you want to do now?" I ask, staring up at the bell tower above us. Despite the promising dog hair—and the evidence still stuck to my shoe—we haven't found any other clues about Cat in the last few blocks.

Daphne shrugs.

"You want to look inside the cathedral?" I ask. "That guidebook I read said it's really nice inside."

"No, I'm tired," Daphne tells me.

"It's from staying up late reading about vampires that don't exist."

This time, Daphne doesn't rise to the bait. "Whatever," she says with a shrug. "I just want to go home."

Sixteen

I walk Daphne back to Last Chance Gulch and then turn left.

Daphne stops. "You're not coming home?"

"You go ahead," I tell her. "I want to look around some more."

She glances away, considering this. Then, her eyes return to me. "Okay. See you later."

"Yeah."

I continue up the street and enter the pedestrian mall at the top of the gulch. I pass the Parrot and consider treating myself to a hot fudge sundae, but decide to skip it this time. The truth is, I'm feeling a little guilty. I shouldn't have given Daphne such a hard time about the vampire books. Girls, well, they just can't help themselves about some things, and I guess that handsome, misunderstood vampires are one of them.

So, instead of going into the Parrot, I walk another couple hundred yards to the Helena Public Library.

The library is pretty new and it's, well, fantastic—all airy with open wood beams and sunlight streaming in. Just inside the main door, on my left, sits a porcelain bear plastered in old book jackets instead of fur. Other statues sprout up from book-cases all around the main floor.

I spot the sign for the children's and young adult section in the back and make my way to it. A librarian at a desk looks up at me.

"Hello."

"Hi," I tell her.

"Need a good book today? We've got plenty," she says, waving her hand around her.

I smile. "I'm covered. Thanks. I came for my friend. You don't happen to have *Vampires in Hollyweird*, Book 7, do you?"

She gives me a sympathetic frown. "You know. We ordered four copies of that. Then, we ordered four more. We just can't keep them in—and there's a huge waiting list."

"Shoot."

"Did you try Montana Books and Toys?"

"Sold out."

"I'm sorry."

"Okay. Thanks."

I turn and start to walk away.

"Wait a minute."

I turn back to the librarian.

"Just let me check something," she says.

While I wait, she quickly types something on her keyboard and studies the result. Then, she picks up her phone and punches three numbers. "Nancy. Trish here. You processing any copies of *Vampires in*

Hollyweird, Book 7?" The librarian—Trish, apparently—pauses a moment and says, "Sure. I can hold."

While we wait, Trish raises her eyes to me and asks, "Is your friend a fast reader?"

"She finished the last one in two days."

"Well, that's pretty—" Trish stops to listen to the phone and her face brightens. "Oh, that's great. I'm sending someone over."

She hangs up and glances around to make sure no one can hear. "We're not supposed to do this," she whispers, "but the next person on the waiting list hasn't been showing up for her turn. If your friend can read Book 7 and return it by the weekend, you can have it."

"Sure! With Daphne, that's no problem."

"Good," the librarian says, satisfied. "You're going to earn big points for this, aren't you?"

I grin. "You can say that again."

Clutching Daphne's book, I stroll lazily toward home. Looking at the huge sky above—and I know it's a cliché, but Montana really does have a *big sky*—I just breathe deeply and try to enjoy the moment. As much as I like hanging out with Daphne, sometimes we need a break from each other. I guess it's like that with everyone except maybe a pet dog or snake...or fish. Yeah, it's hard to imagine a fish getting on someone's nerves, isn't it?

But I'm also glad to have some time alone

to consider what we've learned about Governor Rickson's dog. Strolling down Last Chance Gulch, I try to summarize what Daphne and I have discovered so far about Cat's disappearance. Here's the list I come up with:

1. *Cat was definitely with Governor Rickson before he disappeared. People saw them leave the Mercantile together two mornings ago, Wednesday.*

2. *Cat definitely disappeared somewhere in the three- or four-block stretch between the Merç and St. Helena's Cathedral.*

3. *At least one suspicious character was near the scene that morning—the woman with the wolf on her jacket who was getting coffee at the Merc. Okay, maybe she wasn't suspicious, but no one seemed to know who she was.*

4. *Cat wasn't wearing a collar or any other identification.*

That's not a whole lot to go on, but it's more than we had before. I again think about Senator Futzenburg and wonder if he could have been involved with taking Cat.

He's got a motive, I tell myself, but it just doesn't feel right. It's hard to fake the belly laughs he let out when I told him we suspected him. Plus, even though the senator can seem like a bit of a buffoon sometimes, he didn't strike me as mean-spirited.

No, we can strike the senator off the list of suspects.
I keep walking and turn left up Lawrence, churning the rest of the information over in my mind to see if I've left anything out.

Unfortunately, there isn't much. There's that dog Daphne and I saw up near the fire tower, but we agreed that it probably wasn't Cat. More interesting is that dog hair—and dog poop—we discovered on Jackson Street.

Does that have any significance?
I want it to, but I just can't figure it in. I mean, I suppose that could have been Cat's poop, but realistically, there's no way of knowing. If I were on the television show *Bloody Justice*, I'd have Agent Snortowitz (or whoever) run a DNA lab analysis on it. Here in Helena, I'd be laughed out of town if I brought a Zip-lock bag full of fly-covered poop down to the police station and asked them to analyze it.

So what about the dog hair?
At first, I think, the dog hair holds more promise. It's the same color as Cat's fur, for one thing. There was a lot of it, too. That could mean that Cat was in some kind of struggle—maybe as kidnappers tried to wrestle him into a windowless van with fake license plates.

My steps quicken just thinking about it. Then, I remind myself that even though the dog hair was black and white like Cat's, it didn't have the waviness of Cat's. I've seen a lot of Border collies, and I know their fur can come in many varieties from short to long, straight to curly, but Cat's fur was longish and definitely wavey. I mean, I *want* it to be the same as the fur we found, but it just... well, it's not.

"Shoot," I mutter, kicking at a piece of gravel on the sidewalk. And when I look up, I find that I'm already standing in front of my house.

Seventeen

I pause before going in, wondering if I should take Daphne Book 7 of *Misunderstood Vampires That Pre-Teenaged Girls Want to Fall in Love With*. Or whatever the title is. I decide to wait. As I said, it's good to have a little time apart every once in a while. Okay, the real truth is that I think Daphne needs more time apart than I do. She gets cranky sometimes when we're together too much and seems to miss me more if we don't see each other every single hour.

That kind of annoys me, but I've learned not to push the issue. So I decide to go on into my house. No one is home, but I go to the kitchen, kick off my shoes next to the table, and spot a note from Mom.

Slate, Lily needed some exercise, so we went to the park. Be home soon. Love, Mom

I'm a little relieved, because suddenly, I'm feeling tired. Really tired. I decide to head up to my room and flop down on my bed. I try to think more about Cat, to see if I'm overlooking some vital clue about his disappearance, but...

Before I know it, I'm prying my eyes open, staring dumbly out the window.

"Wow," I mumble out loud. "I didn't know it was possible to fall asleep that fast." I don't know how long I've been unconscious, but the sun is hitting the trees at a low angle outside and my brain feels like it's been filled with sludge. I mean, naps are supposed to make you feel *more* awake, but right now, I feel like someone walloped me over the head with a fifty-pound wet beaver.

"Uhhhh," I moan, stretching my arms out above my head.

Chickadees are calling outside my window. I also hear Lily's voice downstairs, so I brilliantly conclude that my mom and sister are back from the park. I don't quite feel like re-entering the World Of The Wide Awake just yet, however, so I glance around the room. My eyes land on Book 7 of *Vampires in Hollyweird*, sitting on the floor next to my bed.

"What the heck," I say, reaching down for it.

I prop my pillows behind my head and, resting the book on my stomach, open to the first chapter.

It's even worse than I thought.

The opening paragraph, in fact, is obviously picking up from a cliff-hanger that must have ended Book 6. And I'm not talking about a *metaphorical* cliff-hanger, either:

Cristoff reached his arm down toward Constance, who clung to the lone tree root

*that separated her from the deadly chasm,
a chasm that plunged even deeper than her
passionate feelings toward him.*

*"Hang on!" Cristoff shouted, stretching his
fingertips even further toward her.*

*"I-I cannot!" Constance breathed. "It's too
late. Forget about me Cristoff. Live your life
and do not regret our moments together!"*

"If you die, then they win!" he called back.

"Oh, *please!*" I say, suppressing a laugh. Who
gives speeches like this when they are dangling
over a cliff, about to plunge to their deaths?
And what kinds of names are those? Cristoff?
Constance? Who would be caught dead naming
their kids that?

Vampire parents, I guess—who, if you want to
get technical, actually *are* dead.

I keep reading:

*"Just take my hand," Cristoff pleaded. "I
have almost got you!"*

"It's no good!" Constance gasped. "I-I-I-"

*Cristoff watched in horror as Constance's
fingers began slipping from the tree root.*

*And suddenly, his love for her unleashed
a primal surge of hormones flushing through
his body. His muscles pumped up to twice their
normal size. The nails of his toes lengthened*

into curving claws and he let out a cry older than the time when primordial ooze first covered the earth.

As Constance lost her grip on the root, her lifeline, Cristoff threw himself over the side of the cliff and seized her around the waist. At the same instant his nails clawed at the cliff face, sending rocks and debris plunging into the abyss below.

"AAAAAAAA!" he wailed, desperate to save the only being he had ever loved.

Somehow his claws held onto the cliff face. With a strength even he did not know he possessed, he began climbing inch by inch to the top of the cliff, Constance held firmly in his muscular embrace.

It is too much. I drop the book and surrender to a fit of "muscular" guffaws and giggles.

"What are you doing, Sate?"

I look over at the doorway and see Lily studying me curiously.

I sit up and motion her over. "Just reading a funny book."

She hurries to my bedside. "Can you read it to me?"

"Sorry, Lily. This isn't really a book for you. Let's go downstairs and see Mom."

"But I want you to read me a book."

"I'll give you a piggyback."

She grins. "Okay."

Another tough negotiation completed, she climbs up behind me and throws her arms around my neck. I choke. "Not so tight!"

She loosens her grip, and we careen out of my room and down the stairs. I make sure to bump her against the wall, saying "Whoops! Whoops!"

By the time we get to the kitchen, she is cackling like a duck.

"Hi there. Did you have a nice nap?" Mom is peeling an apple for Lily, who absolutely refuses to eat a peel of any kind.

"Yeah, I guess."

"You and Daphne must have had a busy morning."

"We met the governor," I tell her.

She stops peeling and studies me to see if I am joking.

"We did!"

"You mean that you saw him walking around?"

"No, we went to his office to ask him when he'd first noticed Cat missing."

Mom sets her peeling knife down, astonishment on her face. "And he was there? He talked to you?"

"Well, yeah." I am as impressed by this as Mom is, but I play it cool like it's no big deal.

Mom shakes her head and then picks up her knife to resume peeling. "Wow. That's amazing. Did you learn anything?"

"We did," I say, "but it didn't really help us. We still don't know what happened."

"Well," she says. "I still think Cat will turn up somewhere. What's that smell anyway?"

Mom turns to Lily. "Do you need to poop?"

Lily shakes her head—which may or may not mean anything.

Then, I spot my shoes where I'd kicked them off under the kitchen table. "Oh, sorry," I say. "I stepped in something today."

Mom makes a face. "Well, get them out of here—and leave the door open to let in some fresh air!"

Eighteen

Lily comes with me as I take my 'soiled' shoes outside, and my shoe-cleaning project quickly turns into a game of Soaking Your Sibling. Lily isn't quite as skilled at the game as I am, but I 'accidentally' trip and fall a few times, and soon we are both wetter than sponges.

Mom brings us out some towels and we both go in to put on dry clothes. Dinner won't be ready for an hour or so, so I decide this might be a good time to deliver the vampire book.

"I'm going to Daphne's," I tell Mom as I put on my sandals.

"Don't stay too long."

"I won't."

When I reach Daphne's house, I again hear music. Even though I'm hearing only the violin part, the tune sounds vaguely familiar. I wait until I hear a break in the music before knocking on the door. Daphne's mom, Theresa, again answers.

"Um, sorry," I tell her. "I keep interrupting you."

Theresa smiles. "Don't worry, Slate. There's just a couple of tough spots in the *1812 Overture* that I'm feeling insecure about."

"That was the *1812 Overture*?"

"It's a very famous piece. I'm sure you've heard it before. It's the one where the cannons all fire at the end."

"Oh yeah," I say, my brain clicking.

"It's the big finale tomorrow night. You're still coming to the concert, aren't you?"

"We wouldn't miss it," I tell her.

Theresa smiles. "Good. I need all the moral support I can get. Anyway, you're probably here for Daphne."

Without waiting for my confirmation, she calls up the stairs. "Daphne! Slate's here."

"Okay!" I hear Daphne's voice call down.

"Thanks," I tell Theresa, and head for the stairs.

I half expect Daphne to be hanging upside down again, and I have to admit, I wouldn't mind another peek at her belly-button, but no luck. She's sitting at her desk, typing on her laptop computer. And yes, Daphne does have a computer while I do not. It's a sore point between me and my parents, but they tell me every hour I spend online destroys approximately one billion and forty-seven brain cells.

What-ever.

Anyway, as I enter Daphne's room, I hide the vampire book behind my back. "What are you doing?" I ask innocently. "Posting a review of Book 6 of *Vampires in Hollyweird?*"

Daphne swings around and gives me her irritated frog look. "No. I already did that. For your information, I was trying to find if there was any news on Cat."

"Oh," I say, suddenly forgetting my plan to surprise her with Book 7. "Did you find out anything?"

"Actually, the police are beginning to suspect foul play."

"What kind of foul play?"

"Well, they think someone may have taken Cat."

"Gee," I say, laying on the sarcasm. "What an idea."

Daphne rolls her eyes. "Yeah. Yeah. I know you thought of it first, but—"

Suddenly, she stops. "Why is your arm behind your back?"

"No reason," I say. "So what do the police think happened?"

"Slate, are you hiding something?"

She stands up and walks toward me. I back up, but my legs bump into her bed. She reaches around me.

"Slate, what have you got?" she demands.

I try to squirm away, but she grabs me around the waist and wrestles me to the floor. The book flies out of my hand.

Nineteen

Daphne lets out a loud squeal. "SLATE! WHERE DID YOU GET IT?"

I can't hide the grin on my face.

"My top-secret connections."

Daphne seizes the book and checks the spine. "You got it from the library? They've got like a ten-year waiting list!"

"Like I said, I have special connections. But you have to read it in the next two days and return it, okay?"

"As if that's a problem!"

Before I know it, she throws her arms around me and gives me a big squeeze. I am so shocked, I don't even have time to hug her back. I'm thinking, though, that I need to get her books much more often.

To keep Daphne from hearing my thundering heart, I say, "Tell me about Cat."

We get back up off the floor and, clutching Book 7, Daphne returns to her desk chair. I stand over her and try to ignore the peach-smelling scent wafting up from her hair and the soft skin of her neck. Maybe vampires do have the right idea about the neck-biting thing.

Daphne scrolls down through an article on the website of a local news station. "You see, the police have looked everywhere and, even with the whole town on alert, not a trace of Cat has shown up."

I am reading the article myself and say, "They're offering a reward?"

"$5,000."

I whistle. "That's a lot of dog treats. Now, we definitely have to find Cat."

Daphne knows me well enough to know that I don't really care about the money. Not too much anyway. She spins around to face me and says, "I've been thinking about that dog hair we found."

My mouth opens in surprise. I take a few steps back and sit on her bed. "So have I. What are you thinking about it?"

"It's just strange that Cat went missing near there and we found all of this dog fur nearby."

"Don't forget the dog poop."

"Yeah, and the poop, too."

"But," I remind her. "That hair wasn't from a Border collie—at least not from Cat."

"I know. I compared Cat's photo with my pictures of the fur we found. The hair we found was shorter and straighter. Also, Cat had a lot of brown in his coat. We didn't find any brown fur, did we?"

I shake my head. "Just black and white."

"But even though that fur didn't belong to Cat, I just keep thinking it's too much of a coincidence."

I am glad to hear Daphne saying this, because it's the exact same feeling I have. "The problem," I tell her, "is that it doesn't really help us. I mean, even if we went to the police, what are they going to say? They've got bigger things to worry about."

Daphne's shoulders slump. "I know."

We both sit silently for a moment. "Well," I finally say, "maybe someone will still find him."

Daphne looks at me. "Do you really think so?"

"I…I hope so."

"Me too."

Neither of us is convincing. Then, to lighten the mood, I decide to bring up the vampire book.

"So," I tell Daphne. "I read the first few pages of that book."

Her hazel eyes widen and the word 'eagerness' is spelled in 96 font size all over her face. "Book 7? What did you—no, wait! Don't tell me. I want to find out for myself what happens."

"I can't believe you like this stuff," I tell her.

Oops.

The word 'eagerness' is instantly replaced by the word 'defensive'.

"What do you mean?" she says.

"Uh—I mean. I mean it just seems too…too advanced for—"

"Are you calling me stupid, Slate Stephens?" she demands, face turning red.

"No!"

"For your information, my grades are way higher than yours."

They aren't way higher, but I am smart enough to keep my mouth shut at the moment. Instead, I stammer, "No, that's not what I meant."

"Well, what is it then?"

"It's just those...those vampires seem a little silly."

"Silly! As if your books aren't silly! I mean, you still read comic books."

"They're graphic novels," I correct her. "And that's not all I read."

"Like I said, comic books. You're hardly someone to insult *Vampires in Hollyweird.* What don't you like about them, anyway? Not enough blood and gore for you?"

"Oh, c'mon," I say, realizing it's no use trying to backpedal now. "Those names they have. Constance and—what's his name?"

"Cristoff."

"Yeah! Who names people that?"

"They're traditional names from medieval Europe—which you'd know if you bothered to read the books before."

"Yeah, but they don't live in medieval Europe. They live in Hollywood, Cal-i-fornia! And then when Constance falls off the cliff, he suddenly transforms himself into some superhuman—"

"Shut-up! I told you not to tell me!"

"Oh, sorry, but—"

"Slate, why do you always ruin things? Just go away! I don't want to talk you anymore!"

"But I—"

"Go!"

I slink out of the room and shuffle back home. Can I plan a surprise, or what?

Twenty

The next morning, all I want to do is stay in bed and punish myself for being so dumb with Daphne last night. I am such an idiot. Why couldn't I just keep my mouth shut about that stupid book? Would it really hurt me to let Daphne believe it's the greatest story ever told? Today, I decide, I'm going to lie in bed until my body decays into a lump of compost. That's all I deserve.

Dad, though, has different ideas. "C'mon," he tells me. "We're going for a hike."

By noon, he and I are slogging up a canyon north of Helena, looking for a place to dig one of those earthquake fault scarp trenches I told you about before. As we hike, I debate asking Dad about my troubles with Daphne. He is a guy, after all, and being older, is supposed to have some kind of wisdom about these things. Right? Just as I'm about to open my mouth, however, my dad suddenly spots a perfect place to dig. My opportunity to talk vanishes, and my dad gets so excited looking over the fault area that we don't get home until after six o'clock.

Mom is not pleased.

"Nice of you two to show up," she tells us. "The concert starts at 7:30 and I wanted to get good seats.

Now, we'll have to hope that Len and Daphne save us a spot."

Mom is pretty patient about being a geologist's wife. She rarely gives Dad any flack about his extended field expeditions and unpredictable schedules. Tonight, though, I can tell we've crossed the line.

"I told you this was a special occasion," Mom says. "It means a lot to Theresa, so get cleaned up you two."

I start to point out that Mom is often late for things, but somehow this just doesn't seem like the right time.

Instead, Dad and I trade guilty looks, while Lily shouts, "I'm ready!"

"Aren't you special." I grumble at her.

"I am special!" Lily says.

"Move!" Mom commands me.

I head up the stairs to get ready, but without much "vim and vigor". Don't get me wrong. The concert sounds fun. What I'm not looking forward to is facing Daphne. I've made Daphne angry lots of times before, but this time I'm not sure she's going to forgive me.

I get showered and dry off, and start to get dressed. Mom knocks and then enters my room as I'm tugging on my shirt.

"You look nice," she tells me, walking over to my dresser. "I think I may have mixed up some of Dad's socks with yours."

"Mom, do I have to go tonight?"

She's rummaging around in my top dresser drawer. "Yes, you have to go."

"But I really don't feel like it."

"Ah-ha!" She pulls out a pair of size 12 white athletic socks. Then, she turns to me, "Slate, I thought you were looking forward to this concert."

"I was, but..." I try to think of some good reason for my change of heart, but can only come up with the old stand-by. "I don't feel that well."

She steps closer and does what every parent always does—puts her hand on my forehead. "Do you feel sick?"

"Um, not exactly. Maybe a little."

Her eyes meet mine. "Slate, I really want you to come. The Helena Symphony summer concert is famous all over the state, and it was a big honor for Theresa to get invited to play in it."

"I know," I tell her. "I'm just really tired."

Mom frowns. "I should have made your dad promise to bring you home earlier."

"It's not his fault."

Mom ignores my accidental pun and gives a big sigh. She turns her eyes toward my window, thinking. "Well, what about this. You rest up here for a while and then meet us there during inter-mission—about nine o'clock. The second half of the concert should be the most exciting anyway."

"Can I ride my bike?"

"Yes, but make sure you wear your helmet and turn your bike light on. It might be starting to get dark by then."

"Okay."

Mom, Dad, and Lily leave, and I plonk down on the living room couch, feeling guilty and relieved at the same time.

Maybe Daphne will have forgiven me by the second half of the concert. Or maybe she'll realize she misses me after all.

I'm not counting on that, but the possibility gives me hope. I close my eyes and realize I am actually pretty tired after trucking around with Dad all day. My mind swirls into a doze and when I open my eyes again, I can tell that evening is definitely on its way. I trot into the kitchen to look at the clock.

8:30.

"Perfect," I say out loud. I calculate that if I leave soon, I should arrive just as the concert's second half is starting. That way, if Daphne is still mad at me, we won't be forced to talk to each other.

In the mudroom, I slip into a light fleece jacket and strap on my bike helmet. Then, I go out and unlock my bike. I quickly debate switching on the bike light attached to the front handlebars. The sun looks like it's about to drop behind the distant mountains, but there's still plenty of light in the sky. One of the cool things about Montana is that in summer, it doesn't get totally dark until after 10 p.m. It's like being in Alaska or something.

I leave the light off, mount up, and then begin coasting down Lawrence Street. The concert is being held over at Carroll College, at the base of a big sloping lawn on the north side of campus. I have several ways to get there, but decide to follow Lawrence across Park Avenue and then cut left.

Traffic is thin, probably because everyone is at the concert, and in no time I reach the Great Northern Town Center. By the time I pass the carousel and new science center, I can already hear symphony music drifting toward me.

I guess they're moving faster through the program than I thought, I tell myself.

Hurrying now, I pedal through the pedestrian/bike tunnel that cuts under Lyndale Avenue.

And that's when I see it—the dog.

The evening light is starting to fade, but even from a hundred yards away, I can tell that it's a Border collie. It looks a lot like the dog Daphne and I saw a couple of days ago. In fact, I'm pretty sure it's the same dog. Still, I think, it might not be the governor's dog, so I slow down and shout, "HEY, CAT!"

The dog is busy sniffing at a shrub, but when he hears my voice, his head pops up, eyes in my direction. An instant later he takes off, running away from me toward the Carroll College campus.

I crunch down on the gear shift and pedal hard after him.

Unfortunately, the dog doesn't follow the bike path. He cuts up left toward the college buildings. My tires spit tree bark as I race through a landscaped area, trying to follow. I hop a curb, cross a road, jump the curb on the other side, and...lose sight of him.

I slow and dismount, walking my bike. I want to call "CAA-AT", but that's what seemed to scare him in the first place. So instead, I just proceed slowly, looking all around me. From over where the concert is, I hear the orchestra end one symphony piece, followed by a wall of applause. Moments later, another piece begins. I really do like symphony music and am feeling bad about not being there, but I tell myself that finding Cat is more important.

The Fortin Science building—not to be confused with the place I'm taking my science class back in the Town Center—is now on my right as I keep pushing my bike forward, and I study every tree and bush for signs of the dog. Then I see him up ahead, investigating the base of a little octagonal-shaped observatory.

Seeing him again, I am growing more certain that this isn't just any dog. I am almost positive now that this is Cat. Even in the dim light, the dog looks like all the photos of Cat I've seen before.

And if it isn't Cat, why is he trying so hard to get away from me?

In a more soothing voice, I call, "Hey, Cat! Good doggy!"

But the dog again startles and bolts up ahead, zipping left around the corner of a long building that looks like a dormitory. I hop back on my bike and resume the chase. By the time I round the building, I've lost him again.

"Shoot!" I say out loud.

The clouds on the horizon are starting to turn a spectacular purple color, with just hints of orange in the sky beneath them. It really is starting to get dark, and I can feel frustration building in me. Not only am I missing the concert, I am rapidly losing my only chance to find the governor's dog.

I switch on my bike light and slowly begin pedaling around the central part of campus. I pass by a fountain and circle around the entire dorm building. Still, I don't see a sign of Cat.

I'm closer to the concert now and clearly hear some familiar strains of music starting up. They are the same notes I heard Daphne's mom practicing at her house.

"Oh no!" I whisper. "The *1812 Overture!*" This is the last piece of the concert and I've almost missed the entire thing!

I stop in front of St. Charles Hall—the big, ivy-covered brick building they always show in photos of Carroll College—wondering if I should forget about Cat. If I hurry I can still catch most of the last musical number of the concert. I don't want to give up on Cat, but it's been almost ten minutes since I caught a glimpse of him, and he's probably long gone by now. Reluctantly, I decide to abandon my search and start heading toward the concert area.

Then, up ahead, I see movement.

Twenty-One

It's Cat.

I keep my mouth shut this time and pedal steadily toward him. Like all dogs everywhere, this dog is sniffing at something. No, I realize coming closer, he's *chewing* on something he's found under a hedge in front of St. Charles Hall.

I pull to within fifty feet of him, quietly stop, and lay down my bike. In the background, I can hear the string section moving through the slower, central part of the *1812 Overture*. Then, the pace quickens as the horns and violins move into the piece's most familiar theme.

Uh-oh, I think. I know enough about the *1812 Overture* to know that things are about to get very loud.

I move forward, hoping to grab Cat before that happens.

Twenty feet away, I softly say, "Cat?"

He lifts his head and again stares at me, a bone in his mouth.

"It's okay, Cat. Bring that bone over here so I can give it a good sniff."

The dog's tail wags and he looks like he's actually about to walk my way.

Of course, that's when the first electronic cannons fire, and I swear, they are so loud, it sounds like World War III breaking out.

"Cat!" I holler.

It's too late. Terrified, the dog first bolts in my direction, but sees I'm blocking his way, and spins around and dashes back toward the music.

I race back to my bike, jump on, and tear after him.

In a moment I can see him, running up ahead of me toward the far end of St. Charles Hall. Beyond him, much closer now, the Helena Symphony, led by the brass section, is playing louder and louder, filling the air with a spectacular noise. I ignore it, darting and weaving as I follow Cat down through some trees and past a little cave.

Bells start ringing, and still I follow him. I almost crash into a tree, but touch my foot to the ground like a motocross rider taking a turn, and barely manage to miss it. Then, I jump the curb down onto the parking lot that separates St. Charles Hall from the concert area straight ahead. Cat is flat-out now and so am I, pedals spinning as fast as airplane propellers.

As if urging us on, the orchestra builds to a fever pitch. Bells are ringing and horns are blaring and strings are, well, *stringing*. At the far edge of the parking lot, I see a row of people standing, looking away from me and down the hill. There is a gap between some of them, and I watch Cat disappear through it and over the edge of the hill. Without hesitation, I race after him. As I fly through the gap and over the edge onto the downward slope, an astonishing scene spreads out before me. All around, thousands of people are spread across and down the hillside sitting on blankets and chairs. At the bottom of the hill, the orchestra thunders away on a brightly-lit stage, the conductor waving his arms wildly, urging them on. Speakers set up across the hillside amplify the noise so that it's coming from all directions.

Right then, the electronic cannons again fire, making me feel like an infantry soldier descending towards my death. I see Cat up ahead tearing down the hill along a wide central aisle of grass and I follow. As we speed down the hillside, waves of faces turn to stare at us, but I only partly notice. All of my attention is on the dog in front of me.

We keep plummeting down the hill. I am gaining on Cat, but losing control of my bike as my tires bounce and chatter over holes and ruts. Approaching the bottom of the hill, I've almost caught up to Cat. The entire Helena Symphony and its conductor are now right in front of us, blasting a wall of sound into our faces—and blocking our way. I keep my eyes on Cat, trying to guess if he's going to turn left or right.

The answer, it turns out, is neither.

When we reach the bottom of the hill, six rockets launch into the sky from either side of the stage. As red, white, and blue colors burst overhead and sticks of dynamite explode above us, Cat screeches to a halt.

Desperately, I swerve to the right, my left pedal grazing the dog's tail. Unfortunately, my move puts me on a collision course for the center of the symphony stage. It's too late for me even to lay the bike into a slide, so I hit the brakes.

It's not enough.

The bike's handlebars collide with the edge of the stage just as the symphony blasts the final notes of the *1812 Overture* and multicolored fireworks fill the sky with rainbow light. I do a front-flip over the handlebars and roll like a human bowling ball across the stage, smashing into the legs of the conductor.

He goes down like a giant bowling pin and sends the podium crashing forward, where it just misses the First Violin player. Half the string section leaps to its feet and out of the way as chairs and music stands crash and tumble and sheet music flies into the air.

As the final notes of the concert ring in the air, I lie on the stage, dazed, staring up at starbursts of light filling the night sky above. The roar of ten thousand people fills my ears and I grin.

Why?

Because I have just bowled a perfect strike.

Twenty-Two

It is the next morning and I am again lying on my bed—this time thinking about the results of last night's events.

Do you want the good news first, or the bad news?

I've always thought of myself as an optimist so I'm going to give you the good news.

The best news is that I did not manage to break any bones tumbling across the stage. Bruised and battered? A little, but no serious injury. The conductor also escaped harm, probably because he didn't see me coming and stayed nice and relaxed when I bowled him over.

Here's some other good news. The audience—all ten thousand of them—gave me a standing ovation for my heroics. Okay, maybe they weren't giving *me* the standing ovation. Maybe they were giving the symphony a standing ovation. Actually...the more I think about it, it might not have been a standing ovation at all. It was more like people leaping to their feet, gasping in horror as the Human Bowling Ball (me) crashed onto stage, nearly ending the career—and life—of their favorite conductor.

So maybe that second thing isn't really good

news. However, there is one more positive thing to share. After I tumbled across the stage, a couple of responsible concert-goers managed to grab Cat.

So that's the good news. Now it's time for the bad news. Unfortunately, this is going to take longer.

The first thing I should tell you is that the dog I was chasing did *not* turn out to be Cat. I know, I know. You probably figured that out already, but it is a surprise to me. I mean, it *looked* like Cat. So what if it turned out to be a girl dog and was actually some kind of a Cocker Spaniel-pit bull mix and not a Border collie? I guess I made a mistake there, but cut me some slack. It was getting dark and the dog was about the same size as Cat and, well, I really *wanted* it to be Cat.

Oops.

There's some other bad news, too. Even though I escaped injury, my bike, well, it was totaled. My collision with the stage bent the handlebars and front forks. Both wheels crumpled like balsa wood. About the only thing that survived was the stupid headlamp attached to the handlebars. Don't ask me how *that* escaped the demolition.

Also listed under the "Bad" heading, my parents took all of my rights and privileges away forever. No daytime explorations with Daphne. No science class. No computer time. No college education. No food and water.

Okay, I am exaggerating about those last three, but my point is that they were—and are—*very* upset with me. I sort of understand. Looking at it one way, I ruined one of Helena's—actually, Montana's—biggest summer events. An event that hundreds of people had spent months and months rehearsing and planning.

Of course, you could also look at it another way and see that I actually helped provide a *more* dramatic climax to a great concert.

But last night, apparently, my parents didn't choose to see it that way.

"I just don't know what you were thinking," Mom told me as we assembled in my room after the concert.

I tried to explain that I'd seen Cat.

"That wasn't Cat," she reminded me.

"I know, but I *thought* it was. And wouldn't you have wanted me to catch him if it was?"

My mom frowned. "You need to learn better judgement in these situations."

Dad stood in the doorway, silently supporting Mom in her assessment of the evening. Or perhaps he was thinking 'You know, if I'd been Slate, I would have done the same thing.'

Okay, maybe not. And it definitely wasn't the time to ask.

"Well," Mom concluded. "We are very disappointed with your behavior tonight. You should spend the next several days thinking about your decisions and what you could have done differently."

"We want you to write down your conclusions on a piece of paper," Dad chimed in.

"And speaking of writing, you have some big apologies to write," Mom resumed. "Before you go to bed tonight, we want you to make a list. And first on the list should be Theresa. You can get started on them in the morning."

My parents exited the room after that, leaving me to ponder the biggest Bad Thing—how I ruined the concert for Theresa, Len, and Daphne.

And that's something I'm still thinking about this morning, here, lying on my bed. I mean, how can they ever forgive me for what I did? Even if they see I was really trying to do something good?

Daphne especially. As if the vampire book thing wasn't bad enough, Daphne's always telling me I'm too impulsive—that I don't think enough before acting. I guess after last night, maybe I'm starting to see her point.

What if I've ruined things forever between us? What if she never ever speaks to me again?

It gives me an ache in the pit of my stomach. In fact, lying there thinking about Daphne, I realize that they shouldn't call it "heart-ache" when a romance goes bad. Whoever came up with *that* one didn't know anything. Instead, they should call it "stomach-ache", because that's where I'm feeling it right now this minute.

Which is why I am absolutely *flummoxed* when, a few seconds later, Daphne marches into my room.

Twenty-Three

I am so stunned to see her that I can't even get out the words to ask why she's here.

Daphne doesn't help, either. While I watch her from my bed, she silently sets her laptop on my desk and turns it on. She opens the Web browser and quickly types in something. Finally, she turns to face me.

I expect her to launch into an excoriating criticism of my thoughts, feelings, behaviors, and literary tastes, and I brace myself as if I'm about to be battered by a Category Five hurricane.

Instead, Daphne asks, "Have you ever actually seen a Karelian bear dog?"

"*What?*" I am still expecting a verbal beating over last night's events or my review of *Vampires in Hollyweird*, and it takes me a moment to wrap my mind around what she's saying.

"Well, have you?"

Still hesitant, I shake my head. "No."

"Come over here."

I lift myself off the bed and walk stiffly over to the computer screen. Approaching my desk, I keep my eyes on Daphne, half expecting her to take a swing at me. But then, I look down at her computer screen.

There, I see a picture of a handsome black-and-white dog. The dog looks to be about medium size and has a thick chest and pointy ears.

"*That's* a Karelian bear dog?" I ask.

"Yes."

"It looks like..."

"I know," Daphne says. "It looks a lot like a Border collie."

I nod. "I mean, there are differences. The bear dog is stockier, and the ears are shorter. And—"

"And the fur is straighter."

"Yeah," I say, studying the photo closely. "It is. So...?"

I still am not sure where Daphne is going with this, but I'm pretty sure it has something to do with Cat.

"*So,*" Daphne says, "after your dramatic performance last night, I decided to do some more research. I got to thinking about the fur we found over near Last Chance Gulch."

"And you think it might have come from one of those?" I say, pointing to the picture of the bear dog. "What made you even think of that?"

For the next fifteen minutes Daphne explains her logic. At first, I am skeptical, but the more she talks, and the more she shows me things she's looked up on the Internet, the more I become convinced that her theory is correct.

"This is crazy," I say, when she's all finished.

"I thought so, too, at first," she says. "But what better explanation is there?"

"None," I agree. "Cat's been missing four days and no one's seen a trace of him."

"You mean except for your high-speed chase last night?"

I can feel my face flush. "Daphne, I'm really sorry about ruining the concert."

"You should be," Daphne says. "Though technically, you didn't ruin the whole thing. Just the last thirty seconds or so."

"Is your mom mad?"

Daphne's mouth cracks into a slight grin. "A better word might be 'incredulous'. She was actually more concerned that you might have hurt yourself—though I told her it would serve you right."

"*That's* a nice thing to say."

"Well you were a butt."

I had thought I was out of the woods with Daphne, but her comment informs me that I am still surrounded by trees.

My head droops and I say, "Oh, you're talking about the vampire book."

"Hello! Yes, that's what I'm talking about."

"Uh," I mutter, even though it about kills me. "I'm sorry what I said about it."

Daphne puts her hand to her ear. "What? I didn't hear you."

"I said I'm *sorry*," I say with a little more

conviction, even though I'm really not sorry. I mean, I'm sorry for hurting Daphne's feelings. I'm *not* sorry for thinking that books about made-up vampires are pretty ridiculous. I mean first of all, these creatures don't even exist and second of all—

Daphne cuts short my mind rant by saying, "Well, then I forgive you. And it *was* really sweet of you to get me the book from the library."

As she says this, Daphne fixes me with her hazel eyes and suddenly, I want to kiss her again—on the lips this time, not on the ear. Fortunately, more urgent matters stop me from making a repeat fool of myself.

"So what about Cat?" I ask. "If what you say is true, then we're the only ones who know about him."

"I guess we'd better tell someone," Daphne agrees.

That sounds logical, but then I see how absurd it is. "Daphne, even if we *are* right, no one's going to believe a story like that."

She tosses her black hair over her shoulders and sighs. "I know. I wouldn't believe it myself."

"What we've got to do," I say, "is go get Cat ourselves."

"Oh, *sure*," she says, loading the sarcasm. "As if we can—"

Daphne suddenly stops speaking. Our eyes lock together.

"Our dads!" we both exclaim.

Twenty-Four

"Slate, move over!"

Daphne's voice reaches me through a thick fog, and I feel her hands give me a shove.

"Huh?" I mutter, sitting up on the bench seat and forcing my eyes open.

"If you're going to fall asleep, stay on your own side of the seat," Daphne tells me.

"Where are we?" I ask with a yawn.

My dad turns around from the front passenger seat and says, "Just passed East Glacier, heading toward St. Mary's. You have a good nap?"

"I...think so," I respond, examining the trees and mountains surrounding the twisting two-lane road that we're on. After a moment, I pinpoint our exact location—and am again pleased that Daphne and I managed to talk our parents into letting us come.

It wasn't easy. Especially after I'd had all of my rights and privileges as a human being taken away only hours before, Daphne and I had to marshal all of our skills to get them to agree. To succeed, we called our families together and argued like two lawyers in a Hollywood movie. At first our parents didn't believe anything we were saying. They thought we just wanted to go to Glacier Park—which, I admit, was a reasonable assumption.

Step by step, however, we presented our case. I told them of the clues we'd found around town. Daphne showed them the photos of the Karelian bear dogs. We laid out a precise timeline of when the governor's dog had gone missing and how our theory was the only one that made any sense.

In the end, I'm still not sure they believed us. But maybe they believed that *we* believed us. Theresa cast the critical vote. Since my punishment was largely due to my behavior at her concert, I sensed that it was up to her whether or not my parents granted me probation from my jail sentence.

After our closing arguments, though, Theresa looked at my parents and said, "I don't have any objections if you don't."

And that was that. Twelve hours later, Dad woke me up and we ate a quick breakfast. Then we joined Daphne and Len in the old International Travelall that served as OFGOV—the Official Field Geology Operations Vehicle. The Travelall is forty years old and rumbles and rattles like a military transport plane. In fact, it is almost as *big* as a transport plane, with three rows of bench seats and a storage area stuffed with gear in the back. It gets terrible mileage—something like four gallons to the mile—but right now, I don't care. I am just happy to be driving to Glacier Park.

Lowering my voice, I tell Daphne, "I still can't believe we talked our dads into letting us come."

"I know," she murmurs back. "We should be lawyers when we grow up."

"Sounds boring."

We ride in silence for a few moments. Then, I say, "You know, you never told me why you decided to do a Web search for Karelian bear dogs in the first place."

Daphne thinks. Then, she answers, "Actually, it was your doing."

Confusion tweaks my face.

"It was the sight of you barreling down through the concert crowd after that dog," Daphne explains. "When I spotted you coming down that hill, I knew right away what you were doing."

"You mean, you thought it was Cat running in front of me?"

"Well, I didn't know for sure. But I thought it was possible—especially after we'd seen the dog up near the fire tower. Of course, after the concert and up-close, it was obvious that that poor little dog you almost ran over wasn't a Border collie, but in the dim evening light, yes, I could see why you thought it might be."

"Okay..."

"Well, that made me realize how easy it is to mix up a dog—especially a medium-sized black-and-white dog."

"Go on."

"Well, that got me thinking about that fur that we found."

"You mean that *I* found."

Daphne gives me her irritated frog look. "Fine. That *you* found. And I remembered that article about the grizzly bears in Glacier and how they were using Karelian bear dogs to train the bears to stay away from people."

"Okay..."

"And that made me wonder just what a Karelian bear dog looked like. Of course, once I saw a picture of them, I started getting other ideas. That's why I called the *Helena Gazette* and talked to the reporter who's been writing the stories about them."

"And he told you the bear dogs were brought up from Idaho. You looked at a map and saw that Helena was right between Idaho and Glacier Park."

"That's right. And then I remembered the people we talked to in the General Mercantile. A couple of them mentioned a stranger, the woman with the red jacket that had a picture of a wolf on it."

"Another mistaken identity."

Daphne grins. "Exactly. I realized that it might not be a wolf. It might be a dog instead. As soon as the light bulb went on, everything just fell into place. I figured the woman probably stopped for coffee at the General Merc and was driving a big vehicle, or even pulling a trailer to hold her dogs."

"And a big vehicle would be easier to park on Jackson Street than on Last Chance Gulch," I add.

"That's right. And if there was a car full of dogs only a few yards away, there's no way Cat isn't going to rush over and say hello. Meanwhile, Governor Rickson just assumes Cat is by his side and keeps on walking."

I have to admit I'm more than a little impressed by how Daphne put all of these pieces together. But there's still one important part of the story that could blow the whole thing apart.

"But," I say, echoing both our thoughts. "Just because Cat went over to say hello to the Karelian bear dogs doesn't explain how he ended up getting in the car—"

"—or trailer."

"—or whatever with them."

Daphne nods. "I know. But what have we got to lose?"

We don't realize it, but the answer to that question turns out to be "Everything."

Twenty-Five

❀

We stop at the little village of St. Mary's to fill up the OFGOV's enormous gas tank. Then, instead of turning left onto the Going-to-the-Sun Road like most of the tourists do, we continue north along the east side of the park, through Blackfeet Indian reservation lands. This is one of my favorite parts of the drive. To our left rise the first large mountains of Glacier National Park. To our right, the landscape features low aspen-covered ridges that quickly flatten out into shortgrass prairie.

Soon enough, we slow for the town—if you can call it that—of Babb. Len hangs a left and we head directly into the heart of the mountains, up the Many Glacier Valley. For the first few miles we are still on Blackfeet reservation lands. On one side of us runs a clear mountain stream while on the other we pass houses, trailers, and a few cows. Then, we reach a dam and a large reservoir, Lake Sherburne. On cue, we pass a sign that says "Welcome to Glacier National Park."

Immediately, a fresh burst of excitement flows through me. Up ahead, I can already see the stunning peaks of the Many Glacier Valley.

"Look, there's Mt. Gould!" Daphne exclaims, pointing to the valley's most distinctive peak.

"There's Mt. Grinnell!" I say, nodding toward a huge massive directly ahead.

"There's Swiftcurrent," Daphne counters, pointing to a distant pyramid-shaped peak.

The mountains are like old friends. We've climbed many of them with our families and can name practically every feature in the valley. The reason, of course, is that Many Glacier Valley is a geologist's dream. About 170 million years ago, the Rocky Mountains were formed when one continental plate began sliding up and over another one to the east. The result is a thick slab of rock—called the Lewis Overthrust—that is actually much older than the rock underneath it. What that means is that layers and layers of geologic history—very *old* geologic history—are exposed in the park. Even better, the region has been carved, sliced, and diced by wave after wave of enormous glaciers. The glaciers give the valleys a distinctive 'U' shape, but have also sculpted the mountains into dramatic knife-edge geometric shapes.

Daphne asks Len and my dad, "So tell us again why you needed to come up here today?"

Since Len is driving, my dad turns to explain, "You remember last summer, when we were traveling around sampling basalt from the Gunbarrel Event?"

Daphne and I nod. It would be hard to forget. For

six weeks, we drove from Wyoming all the way up into Alberta, Canada searching out this thick layer of black basalt, taking samples. The basalt is the result of a huge outpouring of magma all through western North America that rose from deep in the earth and flowed into upper layers of the earth's crust. Geologists think this happened during the break up of an ancient supercontinent called Rodinia.

"Anyway," Dad continues, "Len dated all of the samples we collected, and just like we thought, the basalt is about 780 million years old everywhere we looked."

"So why did you need to come up here?" Daphne asks.

Len and my Dad give each other annoyed looks. "Well," Dad says, returning his gaze to us, "one of the *so-called* reviewers of the paper we wrote said he wanted to see even more data points."

"Geez," I say, "you had a like a million of them already, didn't you?"

"Yeah," Dad says with a sigh. "But we thought we'd better go ahead and get a few more, and we thought it would be fun to date the huge basalt dike that rises up into the Garden Wall behind Iceberg Lake."

"I know that one!" Daphne exclaims. "It looks like a giant black chimney rising up through the rock."

"So that's why we're here," Dad concludes.

But Daphne and I both know that even geologists

are not immune to the grandeur of Many Glacier Valley. I have no doubts that one reason our dads do so much work here is because they keep looking for reasons to come back. Dad has even said that Glacier is the main reason he came to Montana to be a professor. I totally get that. I think that Daphne does, too. Just seeing this place makes me feel like I'm home again.

About halfway along Lake Sherburne, we pass a National Park Service entry station. Len brings the Travelall to a halt, and the ranger on duty greets our fathers by name.

"It's good to see you back again," she tells them. "What's on the agenda today?"

"We need to collect a few samples."

"Sounds good," the ranger says. "Got your permits?"

Len pats his vest pocket. "All signed and dated."

The ranger smiles.

"Say," my father cuts in, "we heard there are some Karelian bear dogs at work somewhere in the valley. You wouldn't happen to know where they're based, would you?"

"Actually, I do," the ranger answers. "They're camped up at Swiftcurrent Campground. Only, they're probably out working already today."

"Any idea where?" Dad asks.

"My guess is a couple miles up the Iceberg Lake Trail. We had to close that trail because of a grizzly sow and her two cubs. Two days ago, the sow charged a couple of tourists. It was a close call, so they decided to see what they could do with the dogs."

My father lets out a sigh. "Iceburg Lake. Shoot. That's just the trail we were planning to go on."

The ranger says, "Oh, I'm sure it's okay for you to go. You've been in bear country and know what to do. We're just trying to keep innocent tourists from becoming grizzly snacks. Let me radio ahead and let the backcountry rangers know you're coming."

"Thanks," my dad says. "We appreciate that."

Daphne and I look at each other and grin.

Twenty-Six

We continue on up the road, past Apikuni Falls, past the historic Many Glacier Hotel, until we come to the end of the road at Swiftcurrent Lodge. Daphne and I are beaming as we jump out of the Travelall.

"It looks just the same!" Daphne rejoices, twirling in a slow circle with her arms spread wide like a rock star or the Pope, her eyes scanning the awesome peaks surrounding us.

I deeply breathe my favorite air on the whole planet. Crisp. Clear. Smelling of fresh new growth and adventure.

"You two hit the bathrooms and get a snack. Be ready to go in ten minutes," Dad tells us. "Len and I are going to grab a quick cup of coffee."

Unlike the Many Glacier Hotel, which swarms with tour buses and hurried people looking for instant photo opportunities, Swiftcurrent is a more laid-back place—a Mecca for hikers, fishermen, photographers, and mountaineers. It consists of a small restaurant and store, some motel units, and a couple of dozen primitive cabins clustered around shared bathrooms. Across the road from the restaurant, a campground sprawls through woods along Swiftcurrent Creek.

What makes Swiftcurrent so special is its location at two of the best trailheads in the park. Both trails are filled with amazing scenery, but also provide access to spectacular off-trail hikes and climbs. One trail heads west past Red Rock Falls and up over the Continental Divide at Swiftcurrent Pass. The other runs kind of parallel to it, but a bit north. You can branch off of this second trail north through Ptarmigan Tunnel into the Belly River area, or keep following it straight until it dead-ends at Iceberg Lake—which is what we're going to do today.

It is still only ten o'clock in the morning, but feels much later because we've been up for so long. I hear Daphne's stomach grumble and mine joins the chorus. Inside the little store, Daphne buys some trail mix and an apple juice while I opt for a healthier, more balanced meal of root beer, chips and an ice-cream sandwich. We take them to the porch out front and sit down on the steps. All around us, hikers and backpackers are doing last checks on their gear and conferring about their routes on topographical maps. A few minutes later, Len and Dad emerge.

"You ready?" Len asks us.

I lick a last rivulet of ice-cream from my thumb and follow everyone over to the OFGOV. Daphne slings her camera around her neck, and both of us wriggle into our daypacks while Len and my dad hoist their much heavier packs full of hammers, sample bottles, rain parkas, map boards, and other gear. We slam the doors to the Travelall. Len locks the doors. Then we all cut through the cabins and motel area to the trailhead.

"TRAIL CLOSED!" a large sign warns us. Underneath it is posted an explanation about the bear danger.

Dad turns back to us. "I checked with a ranger inside the lobby at Swiftcurrent."

I meet his eyes. "Did you ask about the bear dogs?"

"Yep. He said they've been working about three miles up the trail."

Daphne and I look at each other, smiling. I suppose we should be worried about the actual bears themselves, but Len and my dad are armed with bear spray and noisemakers. Besides, news stories always exaggerate the danger of getting attacked by grizzly bears. We've seen grizzlies lots of times in the park and have never had any trouble with them. Instead of thinking about bears, Daphne and I are thinking about bear dogs—and Cat.

"Do you really think Cat will be with them?" I ask Daphne as we pant up the short, steep first section of trail that emerges out into a stretch of mountain meadow above.

"I don't know," she says, briefly turning back toward me. "I sure hope so. Then again, if they've got Cat, they probably wouldn't bring him out with them while they are working."

"They're probably still wondering where Cat came from," I speculate.

Daphne gives her cute little snort. "Yeah."

But I realize that I'm not really worried about Cat at the moment. We can find him later. What's important right now is that I'm hiking with some of my favorite people in one of the greatest places on earth. I suck in the smells of the mountain meadow, feel the warmth of the sun on my arms, and enjoy the moment.

Does it get better than this?

By now, we are up onto the main section of trail. The trail runs for three or four miles around the base of Mt. Henkel. It's a perfect route, up and out of the trees and a couple of hundred feet above Wilbur Creek down below. From the trail, we can see all of the major peaks in the valley as well as many of the lakes on the valley floor. One reason I'm not worried about bears is because we've got good views of everything. I can't imagine how a grizzly could sneak up on us without plenty of advance warning.

As if he's reading my mind, Len turns to tell us, "We all have to stay sharp today. You two stay close to us, make lots of noise, and keep your eyes peeled. We don't want to end up between a mother grizzly and her two cubs."

"Okay," says Daphne.

"Okay," I echo.

Twenty-Seven

❖

After the first mile, we fall into a hiking rhythm. Our excited chatter dwindles and I enjoy that magical feeling that goes along with setting out on a hike on a spectacular day. It's the feeling before blisters bubble on my toes and sweat stings my eyes, when I still have mountain goat legs that will take me anywhere.

Hiking with geologists, of course, can be both fun and frustrating. It's great to have two professional scientists along to point out interesting rocks and explain land formations. The downside is that sometimes Dad and Len seem to stop every ten steps to look at and talk about something new.

Today, though, the dads seem pretty goal-oriented. Len is bounding ahead at a fast pace that will get us to Iceberg Lake—and the basalt dike above it—in two hours, max. Dad follows close behind Len. Daphne comes next, and I'm bringing up the rear. Having Daphne hiking ahead of me is, well, distracting. Sunlight reveals the brown highlights of her hair. Her tan, strong legs power her along as if they could go forever. I have to keep focusing my eyes on wildflowers or on the peaks around me, because every time I look at her, I trip over a rock or step off the trail. When she hears me stumble, she glances back over her shoulder.

"Walk much?" she asks, a mischievous glint in her hazel eyes.

"Very funny," I tell her.

Except for my attacks of looking at Daphne, I have to admit that it's a perfect day.

Then, after we've been hiking about forty-five minutes, the dreaded affliction sets in.

Geology-itis.

I've noticed my dad scanning some rock outcrops we pass on the trail, as well as the layers showing across the valley at the base of Mount Wilbur. Suddenly, he stops and looks down at a table-sized slab of red sedimentary rock I recognize as red quartzite and shale. The shale was made from mud laid down by prehistoric oceans billions of years ago, and in this piece, I can still see ripple marks from ancient waves.

As I watch, Dad drops his backpack and pulls a little hand lens from his pocket. He kneels down over the rock and examines it closely.

"You know, Len," Dad says looking up at Daphne's father. "I'll bet we could match this rock to the red shale in Siberia."

Len cocks his head slightly. "You mean the shale we heard about at last year's Geophysical Union conference?"

I look at Daphne and begin wriggling out of my

daypack. "Oh boy, here we go."

Daphne sighs and also drops her pack.

For the next ten minutes, Dad and Len talk about the Lewis Overthrust, the breakup of ancient supercontinents, dating techniques, sabbaticals, and grant proposal deadlines.

Daphne and I have heard most of it before, and quickly lose interest. Daphne tries to get a few close-up pictures of wildflowers while I count the number of species I see—shooting star, Indian paintbrush, penstemmon, stonecrop, pearly everlasting—all flowers Mom has taught me over the years. When we've exhausted our flower inventory, the dads still show no sign of wrapping up their discussion.

"Can we go now?" I ask.

"Yeah," Daphne pleads. "We want to find Cat before he dies of old age."

"Just a few more minutes," Dad says, crouched over the slab of red rock with Len.

Daphne rolls her eyes and adopts the Way of the Irritated Frog.

"Can we at least go up ahead?" she asks. "We should be running into the bear dog people if they're around here."

Dad and Len both look at us, and then back at each other. It's obvious that neither of them want to make the decision. It's also obvious they aren't ready to leave.

"We could let them go to Ptarmigan Falls?" Dad suggests.

Len nods and unclips the bear spray from his belt.

"Here, take this. If you see a bear—*any bear*—turn around and hoof it back toward us."

"And don't go past Ptarmigan Falls. Shouldn't be more than a mile. Wait for us there."

"Alright Dad," I say.

"Daphne?" Len asks.

"Yes-we-will-wait," Daphne enunciates clearly.

We are so happy to get moving again, that Daphne and I practically skip the first hundred yards up the trail.

"Whew!" I say. "I thought they were going to talk all day."

"They might," Daphne says. "But at least we can try to find the Karelian bear dog people while they do."

We head up the trail at a fast pace—even faster than we were going before Dad and Len stopped to discuss their geological futures. After five minutes, we hop over a little trickle of a stream that crosses the trail and, a hundred yards later, enter a wooded stretch, with aspens and conifers growing on each side of us. As we pass through another small clearing, however, I halt so abruptly that Daphne smashes into my back.

"Slate!" she shouts. "What are you do—"

Then her voice chokes off.

Twenty-Eight

Not twenty feet from us, a dark, chocolate-colored bear cub pulls its head out of a huckleberry bush and looks straight at us.

Daphne and I stand frozen, staring back at it.

The cub is already pretty big—about thirty pounds I guess—and it is adorably cute. It looks at us with brown eyes that are more curious than anything else.

But Daphne and I are not saying to ourselves, "Oh, what a cute bear cub."

We are thinking, *Where is the mother?*

"This is not good," Daphne whispers.

The understatement of the year.

We glance all around the clearing, but don't see any sign of Mama Bear or other cubs. And that is the break that we're looking for.

We slowly turn and begin tiptoeing back down the trail toward our fathers, and more importantly, away from the cub. We don't make it five steps when loud splintering sounds erupt in front of us. Thirty feet ahead, the largest mammal I have ever seen crashes through the trees onto the trail.

Mama Bear.

The enormous sow is huffing loudly and staring

in our direction. Even from thirty feet away, we can smell her ripe, berry- and carrion-flavored breath wafting around us. Then, in a move that would intimidate a World Wrestling Federation champion, she stands up on her hind legs.

I know what she's doing—trying to get a better look at us. Grizzlies are notorious for having poor eyesight. Unfortunately, my knowledge of her behavior doesn't help me right now. It makes me want to pee my pants.

Daphne and I remain paralyzed. Daphne reaches for her bear spray, but we're not under any illusions. Sometimes bear spray works and sometimes it doesn't. When two people are between Mama and one of her cubs, I'm guessing that the bear spray, well, just might not be all that effective.

Daphne and I don't utter a word. I do, though, slowly reach for Daphne's arm and pull her a step to our right, toward the trees on the downslope side of the trail.

Mama Bear growls and falls heavily down onto her front paws. She bounces up and down like a pile-driver, and I can feel the ground shake beneath us. There's no doubt that the mother knows we're here now. She inhales huge sniffs of air through her nose and exhales in short bursts, as if she's spitting out nails. Grizzlies are like most other animals. They don't go looking for trouble and will try to avoid a confrontation, but this bear is clearly UP-SET. I don't know why she hasn't charged us yet, except that maybe she's not exactly sure where her cubs are at the moment.

Then, from behind us, we hear a little yip from the cub.

Mama Bear hears it, too. That's all it takes. Emitting a roar that shatters every nerve in my body, she launches forward. I yank Daphne to her knees and we both curl into the 'bear protection' position—heads down, hands reaching behind to cover our necks.

Even in this position, I prepare for Mama to rip out our spinal cords and use them as chopsticks while she devours me and Daphne like giant sushi rolls. My only request is that she doesn't eat us feet first.

But then, something amazing happens. Before bear teeth tear into my flesh, the loud, throaty barks of dogs surround us. We feel three bodies rush past us toward the bear, and Daphne and I both look up.

What we see is astonishing. Only ten feet from us three black-and-white dogs are holding the mother grizzly, towering to her full seven-foot height, at bay. The grizzly is roaring and dropping to swipe at the dogs, but the dogs deftly leap out of her reach. All the while, they bark furiously, creating a wall of sound that manages to hold back the most fearsome animal in the Rocky Mountains.

Strong hands seize Daphne and me.

"Quick! Get back!" a woman's voice orders us.

We stumble away from the dogs and Mama bear, quickly retreating back into the trees on the far side of the clearing, putting yardage between us and the mammal-on-mammal scuffle.

We hear more roaring and ferocious barking. Then, almost as soon as it begins, it's over. The roaring stops. The woman with us whistles, and two dogs come trotting happily across the clearing. They look like the Karelian bear dogs we saw on the Internet. They might even be the exact same dogs.

"Good job!" the woman tells them, giving each a treat.

Then, a third dog emerges out into the clearing. This one is most definitely *not* a Karelian bear dog.

"Cat!" Daphne exclaims.

The woman looks at Daphne like she is crazy.

"Uh, darling," she patiently says, "I believe that is a dog, not a cat."

"No," I tell the woman. "That's Cat, the governor's dog."

The woman still isn't getting what we're trying to tell her, but before I can explain, Len and my dad come racing up the trail. They scoop us into their arms.

"Daphne!" Len shouts.

"Slate!" Dad says, crushing me. "Are you both all right?"

"What are you all *doing* here anyway?" the woman asks. "Don't you know this trail is closed?"

Twenty-Nine

After our bear encounter, Dad One and Dad Two decide that maybe they should skip sampling the rocks near Iceberg Lake. Instead, we all—Cat, the Karelian bear dogs, and their handler Carol included—make our way back to Swiftcurrent.

It takes most of the hike to explain to Carol just how and why we've ended up here—and for her to tell us how she ended up with Cat. Daphne and I are pleased to learn that a lot of our theory is correct after all.

"I didn't know I had an extra dog until I arrived up here in Glacier a few days ago," Carol tells us. "Just like you guessed, I stopped for coffee downtown in Helena. I let my dogs out to pee and poop, and then tied them to the trailer I haul them around in. After I got my coffee, I undid their leashes, motioned for them to get back into the trailer, closed it up, and we were on our way."

"So you didn't even know Cat was in the trailer?" I ask.

Carol laughs. "I didn't have a clue. I'm guessing he smelled food from my dogs' food dish and went in there to grab a snack."

"Governor Rickson told us Cat is a real garbage hound," Daphne tells Carol.

"I can see that," Carol says. "But imagine my surprise when I pull into Swiftcurrent later that day, open up the trailer, and find that I have an extra dog with me!"

"Did you know who the dog was?" I ask.

Carol shakes her head as we approach the last stretch of trail before reaching Swiftcurrent. "Nope. I didn't recognize the dog. Didn't even know its name. All I knew was it was a Border collie. I did guess that I'd picked him up in Helena, and thought I'd drop him off at the Helena Humane Society when I went back through there next week. Then, when I saw how smart he was, I decided to see how he'd do out on the trail with the bear dogs."

"And?" Daphne asks.

"Well, he turned out to be a natural. He just watched the bear dogs and did what they did. They all seemed to get along, too, so I figured that if no one reported him missing, I'd just make him a part of the team."

"But didn't you see the newspapers?" I ask her, as we reach the motel units behind Swiftcurrent's main building.

"Naw, not while I'm up here at least. Besides," she adds, gesturing to the mountains around us, "who wants to know about the outside world when you're visiting paradise?"

The rest of us laugh. We know exactly what she means.

We decide to stay over at Swiftcurrent that night. We set up our tent in the campground and invite Carol and her pack over for dinner. We stay up late telling stories, and getting to know the bear dogs. She's got five of them altogether, and they really are cool. Strong. Friendly. I can tell why Carol loves working with them.

The next morning, Carol says a sad goodbye to us and Cat.

"I'm going to miss him," she says. "He's a great dog. The governor's lucky to have him—and to have you two to help get him back."

"Well…" is all I manage to say, but Daphne says, "Thank you."

Then, Daphne and I give the bear dogs each a good pet.

"Thank you for saving us," I tell them.

"Believe me, it was their pleasure," Carol tells us. "They love it out here. Do me a favor, though, okay?"

"What?" I ask.

"Pay attention the next time the trail says CLOSED."

"We promise," Dad answers for all of us.

Cat climbs back into the OFGOV with us and together we rumble out of Swiftcurrent, heading toward the East Glacier highway. Once we're back in cell phone range, Dad calls Mom and tells her what happened—leaving out certain details about our near-death experience at the paws of Mama Bear. Mom sounds relieved to know we're okay, and promises to call Theresa and tell her we'll be back in a few hours.

On the drive back, we lavish nonstop petting and treats on Cat, and excitedly hash over the events of the last twenty-four hours. We can tell that both Len and Dad feel majorly guilty for letting us hike ahead of them, but Daphne and I downplay just how close a call we actually had. Together, the four of us decide that once we reach Helena, we should drive directly to the Capitol to return Cat to Governor Rickson.

We're barely back on the Interstate, however, when two State Troopers join us, one in front and one behind.

"Uh-oh!" Len exclaims, glancing down at the speedometer. "What do *they* want?"

Then one of the troopers motions for us to fall in behind him.

Dad chuckles and glances back at me and Daphne. "It looks like we have an official escort. I do believe Mom called some other people besides Theresa!"

Daphne and I both give Cat a hug, and we all barrel happily southbound.

The excitement, though, has barely begun.

When we get off at the Helena exit, the troopers turn on lights and sirens, and our escort quickly turns into a parade. All along the city streets people are standing there waving. Some don't seem to have any idea what's going on, but more than a few have evidently heard the news.

"CAT!" kids scream as we drive past. Daphne rolls down her window so Cat can stick his head out, tongue flapping in the breeze, and acknowledge his fans.

When we pull in front of the Capitol itself, the mayhem multiplies. At least five hundred people are gathered in a crowd to greet us. I count four television station trucks and half-a-dozen radio and newspaper people. As we pile out of the Travelall, Governor Rickson himself steps out of the crowd and Cat rushes to him.

Dozens of strobe lights flash and news cameras hum as the governor kneels down to embrace his dog. Real tears run down the governor's cheeks as Cat nestles up against him. Daphne reaches into her pocket for a tissue.

Almost immediately, the cameras turn toward us and we are battered by questions.

"How did you find him?"

"We heard there was a bear attack!"

"Is it true you paid a ransom to get Cat back?"

Daphne and I do our best to answer, but Governor Rickson rescues us.

"Please everyone!" he says, wading into the mix. "I'm sure these young heroes will be happy to hold a press conference later. But right now, I, Cat, and my family wish to personally thank them for returning Cat to us. And as a small token, I would like to award them with the Citizens' Service Medal for their efforts in reuniting our family. Sheila?"

Governor Rickson turns to his Deputy Chief of Staff, Sheila Russo. She opens a velvet-lined wooden case, and the governor lifts out two bronze medals on red, white, and blue ribbons, and places one around each of our necks.

Off to the side, I see Senator Futzenburger, red-faced, rolling his eyes. I grin. I wonder what his ole Daddy is telling him now?

Thirty

❖

The next week, Daphne and I are kept busy by press conferences, newspaper interviews, and radio appearances. We even get a call from *Highlights for Children* magazine to see if we want to write a story about recovering Cat. The following Wednesday, our families go to the Capitol where, amidst a sea of camera flashes, Governor Rickson hands Daphne and me a check—the $5,000 reward for finding Cat.

Daphne and I have talked about what we want to do with the reward—whether to keep it, give it back, or donate it to some charity. Unfortunately, our moms have also been doing some talking. As soon as the "photo op" finishes, Mom snatches the check from our hands.

"Mom!" I protest.

"College," she replies.

After the ceremony, we all accompany the governor to the executive residence for a barbeque, and we soon forget about our pilfered check. We have a blast playing with Cat, meeting Mrs. Rickson, and getting to know each other better.

Like every politician, the governor has a gift for gab. Out in his backyard, he entertains us with his adventures growing up near Fort Benton and tells us one hilarious story after another.

"You know in my first campaign, when I ran for the House of Representatives, we were so poor we couldn't even afford yard signs. You remember that Betsy?"

Betsy—Mrs. Rickson—is setting out some cold drinks on a nearby table. "I remember," she answers.

"Anyway," he tells us with a wink, "we learned that my opponent kept all his yard signs in a big shed a couple of blocks away. We drove over there at midnight, and discovered that the shed was unlocked. We snatched his signs and planned to throw them away. Then, I got an even better idea. We repainted them! The next day, we had more yard signs up then anybody else!

"Of course," he admits, "my opponent got us back a couple of days later when he pretended he was me on the phone, and cancelled three or four of my big appearances right before the election."

Daphne's mouth hangs open. "Did you still win?"

The governor laughs. "Not that time. I beat him two years later, though, after I got Cat and started taking him out on the stump with me. Cat's been my good-luck charm ever since!"

After our evening with the governor, things get pretty quiet again. The news reporters turn their attention back to the special session on education. My parents lift my "grounded for life" status, and I return to my science class. Best of all, Daphne and I start hanging out again.

A couple of times a week, we go out with our fathers as they start digging the new earthquake fault trench in the place Dad and I found on our last hike. Daphne and I help out as much as we can, carrying buckets of dirt, taking pictures, scribbling notes, and getting water for the crew of workers. We also have plenty of time to explore around Helena. We hit the library almost every day to read and work on our *Highlights* story. Of course, we have to make sure the Parrot stays in business, too.

Throughout all of it, Daphne never mentions the Ear Kiss or my other strange behavior of recent weeks. I don't bring it up either, and hope she's forgotten about it.

One afternoon after hitting the library, though, we decide to walk back up to the old fire tower overlooking downtown. It's a gorgeous day, and the sun has dropped to within a few inches of the mountains to the west. It's that time of day when things just slow down and you can watch the light change colors and shadows stretch across everything.

We chat about our article as we hike up the hill. When we reach the top, we find a grassy patch and sit down. We don't say anything for a moment, just enjoy looking out over one of the greatest places on earth.

Finally, Daphne turns to me and sweeps a lock of

her dark hair back over her ear. My pulse races as she stares at me with her hazel eyes. My heart drumbeats even faster when she doesn't say anything.

"What?" I finally croak.

She blinks and says, "You know, Slate. It's okay if you like me."

"I know that," I say.

"I mean it's okay if you *like me* like me."

"Oh." I swallow hard. "It is?"

She smiles her most dazzling smile—a smile even more dazzling than the one she flashed at that lame receptionist in the governor's office.

"Yes," she says. "It is."

Then, without another word, she wraps her fingers into mine. Together, we lie back in the grass and stare up at the immense Montana sky.

The End

Tail Wags

I am always honored—and a little surprised—that so many people are willing to help me with something that is basically a lot of fun to do. The more I write, however, the more I am convinced that the best books would never happen without the input, ideas, and cooperation of many people. This book is no exception.

At the top of my list are the many people in Helena who gave me access to, and the inside scoop on, Montana's government. At the Capitol, I'd like to thank Governor Brian Schweitzer, Lieutenant Governor John Bohlinger, Secretary of State Linda McCulloch, and the governor's Deputy Chief of Staff Sheena Wilson for so generously sharing their time and stories with me. I am also grateful to State Senator Carol Williams for helping smooth my way to the capital and Deb Mitchell, for providing me with the outstanding tour of the capitol building—and helping me locate the Minority Leader's elusive office!

This book absolutely would not be possible without the generous help, ideas, and patience of Professor James Sears at the University of Montana. Professor Sears not only took me out in the field in an attempt to teach me some real geology, but gave me a wealth of ideas that I incorporated into this book—and kindly read over the manuscript for errors. Thank you Jim!

Additional thanks go to Dr. Charles Jonkel of the Great Bear Foundation for making sure my grizzlies behaved properly; Ray Domer at the General Mercantile for walking me through the back exit; Brian Shovers and Ellen Baumler at the Montana Historical Society for setting the Four Georgians straight; and Bear Management Ranger Bob Adams for checking out the Iceberg Lake trail.

As always, I appreciate the enthusiasm, ideas, and support of my writer's group. Peggy, Jeanette, Dorothy, and Wendy—you all are great! Bruce, thank you for the careful read and comments!

A huge thank you to Kathy Herlihy-Paoli of Inkstone Design for once again turning my work into art, and to fellow author Wendy Parciak and her Border collie Tarzan for patiently facilitating the cover shot.

Thank you to my editor Harold Underdown for helping me sand off the rough edges and helping me see the Big Picture.

Steve Isaacson, what would I do without you and your flyin' website fingers and expertise?

My son Braden is rapidly becoming my right hand in the research department, accompanying me on research trips, giving me his insights, and critiquing my often-misguided ideas. Likewise, my daughter Tessa provided inspiration and dialogue for Lily. My gratitude to my wife Amy, for acting as my guide and final set of eyes on this and other books.

And now, on to further adventures of Slate and Daphne...

HANGMAN'S GOLD

Sneed B. Collard III

One

"**B**utcher Dan, Bad-Luck MacIntyre, and Slippery Slate, the three of you have been tried by this vigilance committee. We find you guilty of the following crimes: murder, larceny, extortion, intimidation, and the use of foul language in front of respectable women. Before I read your sentence, how do you respond?"

Dan, one of the two men next to me, clears his throat and hocks out a fat glob of spit onto the frozen ground. "Ain't got nothin' to say to youse. None of youse got the right to judge us!"

Bad-Luck MacIntyre, the man standing between Dan and me, isn't so composed. His legs are trembling, and snot runs down his nose. "Please! I beg you! Allow me to go to my house and say g'bye to my sweet Martha 'n the kids! They got nobody 'round here. Just grant me one minute to say my farewells. You kin even keep my hands tied."

The man who pronounced our sentence—the Judge—looks back at the twenty other stone-faced men behind him. "Boys?" he asks.

"Let 'em swing," one of the men growls. "We're gettin' cold."

The Judge turns his eyes back to the man and

shakes his head. "Sorry, Mac. Can't do it."

Finally, the Judge looks at me. "Slippery Slate Stephens, you have anything you want to tell us?"

Actually, I do. I want to protest my guilty verdict, demand a lawyer, and ask how I ended up here in the first place. Unfortunately, I am so petrified that my tongue sticks to my throat like a log to a dry creek bed.

The Judge waits an entire four seconds for me to answer, then moves on. "Very well. By order of this Court of Justice, we sentence the three of you to Death by hanging, to be carried out immediately."

The Executioner—a man as big as a slab of granite—steps up from behind us. With cracked, calloused hands, he fits nooses around each of our necks and snugs them down.

"Up on the barrels you three," he growls.

"No! This can't be happening!" my mind shouts, but again, the words can't find my tongue. One by one, we are boosted up onto the wooden barrels. The ropes are pulled taut over the log beam of the gallows above our heads.

The Judge asks us, "Any last words?"

Butcher Dan glares at the crowd before him. "I'll see you all in HELL!"

The Judge nods and the Executioner kicks the barrel out from under him. Dan is lucky. Even though the drop is short, it manages to break his neck, killing him instantly. Luck does not shine so well onto Bad-Luck Mac. He survives the drop, *and is left strangling, his feet kicking wildly only inches above the frozen earth. His desperate, choking squeals send a fresh wave of terror through me and my legs almost collapse of their own accord.*

The Executioner lets out a harsh guffaw. "Now, now, Slippery Slate. No need to hurry yourself," he tells me. "We'll take care 'o you faster than a moose can poop."

The Executioner looks at the Judge. "Ready?"

The Judge nods.

"NO!" I finally manage to scream.

"Yes, sorry son. We've got to get moving."

My eyes snap open.

Instead of a group of stone-faced men, I see the pinkish light of dawn shining through the nylon wall of our tent.

"Too early," I moan, burrowing back into my down sleeping bag.

Dad gives me a playful kick. "Slate, it's almost broad daylight. C'mon. Hot water is on, and we've got a lot of ground to cover before Len and Daphne arrive tonight."

That does get me moving. Not the hot water. Daphne's arrival. It's been almost two weeks since I've seen her. Our families had planned to stay in Helena the entire summer so that our dads could study the earthquake faults in the area. My father finished his part of the work early, though. While Daphne and her family stayed behind in Montana's capital, Dad dragged me down here to the ghost town of Bannack to assist him on a last-minute consulting job—doing some prospecting for a large gold mining company.

"Get dressed," Dad instructs, leaving the tent and zipping the large door behind him. "It's supposed to get up into the nineties today, and I want to beat the heat."

Eighteen minutes, a bowl of oatmeal, and a trip to the outhouse later, I am following my dad on a trail north, away from the deserted main street of Bannack. Within two hundred yards, we pass a pair of tall posts with a log beam mounted on top of them. A shudder passes through me and I stop to stare at the ancient gallows.

Dad also stops. "What's wrong?"

Our rush to get ready had made me forget about my dream, but it now lurches back to me in disturbing detail. "Uh," I tell him. "I had a bad dream last night."

Dad looks from me to the gallows and back again. He grins. "That book about the vigilantes getting to you? Maybe you should read something else."

"That's all I could find," I say.

Still, as we continue hiking past the gallows, I think, *Dad's right. I've got to find something different to read.*

Two

Prospecting for gold isn't nearly as exciting as it sounds. I usually spend the entire day following my father through sagebrush, up over hills, and down into ravines. Every once in a while, Dad stops, turns slowly in circles, and picks up a rock to examine. My job is to take notes, mark locations on a geological map, and collect rock samples until my pack is heavier than I am.

Today, though, we actually get back to our campsite before my pack drags me into the dirt. I have Len and Daphne to thank for that. Even though Dad would like to hike the hills until midnight, my father is also the King of Organization. He wants to make sure our camp is spic-and-span before Len and Daphne show up. By the time I spot the OFGOV—the Official Field Geology Operations Vehicle—rumbling down the gravel road toward us, our camp is so spotless a coyote wouldn't even sniff it.

"Slate!" Daphne shouts, leaping out of the Travelall's door even before Len has turned off the engine.

I have been thinking about this moment for the last two weeks, and have carefully planned how I would greet Daphne. After weighing every option, I concluded that a light punch on the shoulder would be most appropriate. Daphne, though, crashes into me and throws her arms around me.

Her option is better.

"Nice campsite," Len says, sauntering up to us.

Dad shakes hands with him. "The campground manager and I go way back."

"Is that Grasshopper Creek?" Daphne exclaims, looking at the cold, clear trout stream within spitting distance of our tent.

"Yeah," I tell her.

"This is *great!*" she shouts, twirling slowly, taking in the valley and hills surrounding us.

Len and Dad both chuckle.

"What?" Daphne challenges them.

My dad waves his hand, still smiling. "No. No. You're absolutely right. This is great."

"Where do we put our tent?"

"I was thinking over there." Dad gestures to a clear patch of ground on the other side of the picnic table, next to a stand of cottonwoods.

"Why don't you and Slate set up the tent while Andrew and I unload the Travelall?" Len suggests.

"Well," I say, "I was kind of hoping to show Daphne a little of Bannack before it gets dark."

"Can we?" Daphne pleads.

Len and my dad look at each other and Len sighs dramatically. "Go ahead," he tells us. "As usual, we will do all of your chores for you."

We don't bother challenging that insulting remark. Instead, Daphne grabs her camera and we practically skip out of the campground.

"How were the last two weeks in Helena?" I ask as we walk down the dry gravel road. I admit that I don't really care about her answer. I am just enjoying watching Daphne walk next to me again, trying unsuccessfully to keep black wisps of hair out of her face.

"It was great," she tells me.

"Oh." It's not the answer I want to hear. What I *want* to hear is how her life was excruciatingly unbearable because she missed me so much.

"I found out that I got into Yearbook at school," she explains. "And you are *never* going to believe this."

"What?"

Before she can answer, the silent buildings of the ghost town stretch out ahead of us.

Daphne's shoes scrunch to a halt. "Wow."

"Yeah," I tell her. "Bannack isn't like Helena. When it became a state park, they didn't try to make everything look new again. They just preserved the buildings like they were."

"Great light right now." Daphne lines up a picture with the evening sun reflecting off of the ancient buildings. She snaps the shot, checks it, then lowers her camera. "I like this place," she says.

"There used to be a lot more buildings," I tell her, proud to show off what I've learned in the past two weeks. "About 3,000 people lived here right after gold was discovered. Over time, most of the buildings got burned or torn down. This here is the Governor's mansion." I point to a crooked, warped hovel made out of rough-cut wooden beams.

Daphne gives the cute little snort that she gives. "The Governor lived in *that?*"

"Well, remember, this was 1863, and he was only the territorial governor. Montana hadn't become a state yet."

"What's that over there?" Daphne asks, gesturing to a cool-looking wooden structure with multi-pane windows across the front.

"That's the Assay Office. It's where the miners brought their gold to see how pure it was."

"Slate, I *know* what an Assay Office is. Hello? Our fathers are geologists?"

I blush. "Oh yeah."

Daphne smiles and then walks toward a two-story, weathered building with a chimney and bell-tower. "Isn't that the old school house and Masonic Lodge?"

I follow her toward it, puzzled. "How did you know that?"

"Oh..." Daphne stammers. "I think I read something about it somewhere."

"Wait a minute. Have you been here before?"

Now it's Daphne's turn to blush. "Well, yes, but it was a long time ago."

Can I feel any more stupid? Here I am showing off how smart I am, and Daphne probably knows everything I've told her already. "Why didn't you tell me?" I demand.

"I don't know," she says. "You just seemed happy to be giving me the tour."

"Great," I huff, my mood souring.

"Come on, Slate. I didn't know *everything* you told me."

"Only ninety percent? Ninety-nine-point-nine percent?"

"Don't take it that way. I liked hearing it from you."

"Fine," I grunt, following as she keeps walking toward the building.

The schoolhouse/Masonic Lodge is surrounded by a weathered, gray picket fence and sagebrush bushes taller than I am. Still steaming, I push past Daphne and march up to the door. I jerk on the handle and the door squeaks open.

"Are we allowed to go in there?" Daphne asks.

Without answering, I step inside. There, a shiver runs through me. Yellow shades are drawn over the windows, and the setting sun casts an otherworldly glow over rows of wooden desks that have sat undisturbed for more than sixty years. Dozens of slowly drifting dust specks catch the light in the warm, still air.

I hear the door squeak closed behind me. "This

is eerie," Daphne whispers. "Look at that old chalk board on the wall."

I nod silently.

"Geez, can you imagine sitting at these desks for six or seven hours a day?" she continues. "I'll bet teachers back then didn't put up with any wriggling around, either."

I slide into a hard, wooden chair attached to a desk.

"Slate, that's creepy," Daphne tells me. "I mean, everyone who used to sit in those seats is probably *dead*."

Of course, this only encourages me. I raise my hand and say, "Uh, Mrs. Teacher, I have to go to the outhouse! Really. It's Number Two and I have to go *now*!"

Daphne pulls back her lips into her irritated frog look. "You are so *puerile*, Slate."

"I wonder if there's any gum still stuck under the desk?"

Daphne turns away in disgust as I feel around under the desk. I find nothing, so my hands reach down under the chair.

And that's when I touch it. Something jammed into a crack between the seat and the chair frame. Without thinking, I pull it out—a piece of wadded up paper.

"What's that?" Daphne says, stepping over to me.

"It was underneath the chair."

"And you removed it? Do you think that's allowed?"

"It's just a piece of paper," I say, still a little miffed she didn't tell me she'd been to Bannack before. To prove my point, I slap the paper down on the desk, unroll it, and press it flat with my palm. At first I can't tell what I'm looking at. Then I let out a surprised "Huh!"

Daphne leans over so that a lock of her peach-scented hair tickles my neck. "What is it, Slate?"

"It's a map," I say. "It looks like…a treasure map."

To Be Continued…

About the Author

Sneed B. Collard III is the author of more than fifty-five books for young readers including the acclaimed novels *Dog Sense*, *Flash Point*, and *Double Eagle*. In addition to his fiction, Sneed has written dozens of outstanding nonfiction children's books including *Animal Dads*, *Pocket Babies and Other Amazing Marsupials*, *Shep—Our Most Loyal Dog*, and *The World Famous Miles City Bucking Horse Sale*, also available from Bucking Horse Books. In 2006, Sneed was awarded the prestigious *Washington Post*-Children's Book Guild Nonfiction Award for his body of work.

When he is not writing, Sneed can often be found speaking to students, teachers, and librarians across the country. To learn more about him or to set up a school or conference visit, go to his website **www. sneedbcollardiii.com** or the website of Bucking Horse Books, **www.buckinghorsebooks.com**.

Other Selected Titles by Sneed B. Collard III

MIDDLE-GRADE AND YOUNG ADULT FICTION
Dog Sense, winner of the ASPCA Henry Bergh Award
Flash Point, winner of the Green Earth Book Award
Double Eagle, on the state award lists for Kansas, Vermont, and
   Missouri
Slate Stephens Mysteries:
The Governor's Dog is Missing (2011)
Hangman's Gold (2012)

NONFICTION PICTURE BOOKS
Animal Dads
Animals Asleep
Beaks
Creepy Creatures
Our Wet World
Many Biomes, One Earth
The Forest in the Clouds
The Deep Sea Floor
One Night in the Coral Sea
A Platypus, Probably
Wings
Teeth
B is for Big Sky Country—A Montana Alphabet
Shep—Our Most Loyal Dog

NONFICTION MIDDLE-GRADE and YOUNG ADULT
Monteverde—Science and Scientists in a Costa Rican Cloud Forest
The Prairie Builders—Reconstructing America's Lost Grasslands
Pocket Babies and Other Amazing Marsupials
Science Warriors—The Battle Against Invasive Species
Reign of the Sea Dragons

For the latest on Sneed Collard books, check the following:
www.sneedbcollardiii.com *and* www.buckinghorsebooks.com.